P...

STEPH...

and the #1 *New York Times* bestseller

CELL

"If any writer is capable of producing the Great American Zombie Novel, it would have to be Stephen King. . . . *Cell* is hard to put down once you've picked it up. There is no shortage of harrowing scenes. . . . A solid, entertaining read."

—*The Washington Post*

"It's [King's] manic creative energy, [his] crazy headlong non-stop verve, that makes *Cell* a marvel. . . . With his exquisite and unerring knack for just what it takes to keep readers sublimely hooked . . . you realize you're utterly at the mercy of a master storyteller. *Cell* includes some of King's most beautiful writing and affecting characterizations."

—*Chicago Tribune*

"*Cell* [is] the most upsetting and vital novel I've read since Philip Roth's *The Plot Against America*. . . . The horror in *Cell* works on a deeper, more frightening level than as a metaphor for the untenable choices we face when responding to a violent threat. . . . In refusing to reduce experience to sloganeering, King is doing the sort of hard—both difficult and tough-minded—moral thinking that . . . only a few of our political writers and artists have attempted, let alone achieved. . . . [An] engrossing and terrifying story."

—*Newsday* (New York)

STEPHEN KING

A NOVEL

POCKET BOOKS

New York London Toronto Sydney New Delhi

Pocket Books
An Imprint of Simon & Schuster, Inc.
1230 Avenue of the Americas
New York, NY 10020

This book is a work of fiction. Any references to historical events, real people, or real places are used fictitiously. Other names, characters, places, and events are products of the author's imagination, and any resemblance to actual events or places or persons, living or dead, is entirely coincidental.

This Pocket Books paperback edition July 2016

POCKET and colophon are registered trademarks of Simon & Schuster, Inc.

For information about special discounts for bulk purchases, please contact Simon & Schuster Special Sales at 1-866-506-1949 or business@simonandschuster.com.

The Simon & Schuster Speakers Bureau can bring authors to your live event. For more information or to book an event, contact the Simon & Schuster Speakers Bureau at 1-866-248-3049 or visit our website at www.simonspeakers.com.

Manufactured in the United States of America

10 9 8 7 6 5 4 3

ISBN 978-1-5011-2224-8
ISBN 978-0-7432-9672-4 (ebook)

For Richard Matheson and George Romero

The id will not stand for a delay in gratification. It always feels the tension of the unfulfilled urge.

SIGMUND FREUD

Human aggression is instinctual. Humans have not evolved any ritualized aggression-inhibiting mechanisms to ensure the survival of the species. For this reason man is considered a very dangerous animal.

KONRAD LORENZ

Can you hear me now?

VERIZON

Civilization slipped into its second dark age on an unsurprising track of blood, but with a speed that could not have been foreseen by even the most pessimistic futurist. It was as if it had been waiting to go. On October 1, God was in His heaven, the stock market stood at 10,140, and most of the planes were on time (except for those landing and taking off in Chicago, and that was to be expected). Two weeks later the skies belonged to the birds again and the stock market was a memory. By Halloween, every major city from New York to Moscow stank to the empty heavens and the world as it had been was a memory.

THE PULSE

1

The event that came to be known as The Pulse began at 3:03 p.m., eastern standard time, on the afternoon of October 1. The term was a misnomer, of course, but within ten hours of the event, most of the scientists capable of pointing this out were either dead or insane. The name hardly mattered, in any case. What mattered was the effect.

At three o'clock on that day, a young man of no particular importance to history came walking—almost bouncing—east along Boylston Street in Boston. His name was Clayton Riddell. There was an expression of undoubted contentment on his face to go along with the spring in his step. From his left hand there swung the handles of an artist's portfolio, the kind that closes and latches to make a traveling case. Twined around the fingers of his right hand was the drawstring of a brown plastic shopping bag with the words **small treasures** printed on it for anyone who cared to read them.

Inside the bag, swinging back and forth, was a small round object. A present, you might have guessed, and you would have been right. You might further have guessed that this Clayton Riddell was a young man seeking to commemorate some small (or perhaps even not so small) victory with a **small treasure,** and you would have been right again. The item inside the bag was a rather expensive glass paperweight with a gray haze of dandelion fluff caught in its center. He had bought it on his walk back from the Copley Square Hotel to the much humbler Atlantic Avenue Inn where he was staying, frightened by the ninety-dollar pricetag on the paperweight's base, somehow even more frightened by the realization that he could now afford such a thing.

Handing his credit card over to the clerk had taken almost physical courage. He doubted if he could have done it if the paperweight had been for himself; he would have muttered something about having changed his mind and scuttled out of the shop. But it was for Sharon. Sharon liked such things, and she still liked him—*I'm pulling for you, baby,* she'd said the day before he left for Boston. Considering the shit they'd put each other through over the last year, that had touched him. Now he wanted to touch her, if that was still possible. The paperweight was a small thing (a **small treasure**), but he was sure she'd love that delicate gray haze deep down in the middle of the glass, like a pocket fog.

2

Clay's attention was attracted by the tinkle of an ice cream truck. It was parked across from the Four Seasons Hotel (which was even grander than the Copley Square) and next to the Boston Common, which ran along Boylston for two or three blocks on this side of the street. The words MISTER SOFTEE were printed in rainbow colors over a pair of dancing ice cream cones. Three kids were clustered around the window, bookbags at their feet, waiting to receive goodies. Behind them stood a woman in a pants suit with a poodle on a leash and a couple of teenage girls in lowrider jeans with iPods and earphones that were currently slung around their necks so they could murmur together—earnestly, no giggles.

Clay stood behind them, turning what had been a little group into a short line. He had bought his estranged wife a present; he would stop at Comix Supreme on the way home and buy his son the new issue of *Spider-Man*; he might as well treat himself, as well. He was bursting to tell Sharon his news, but she'd be out of reach until she got home, three forty-five or so. He thought he would hang around the Inn at least until he talked to her, mostly pacing the confines of his small room and looking at his latched-up portfolio. In the meantime, Mister Softee made an acceptable diversion.

The guy in the truck served the three kids at the window, two Dilly Bars and a monster chocolate-and-vanilla swirl sof'-serve cone for the big spender in the middle, who was apparently paying for all of them. While he fumbled a rat's nest of dollar bills from the pocket of his fashionably baggy jeans, the woman with the poodle and the power suit dipped into her shoulder bag, came out with her cell phone—women in power suits would no more leave home without their cell phones than without their AmEx cards—and flipped it open. Behind them, in the park, a dog barked and someone shouted. It did not sound to Clay like a happy shout, but when he looked over his shoulder all he could see were a few strollers, a dog trotting with a Frisbee in its mouth (weren't they supposed to be on leashes in there, he wondered), acres of sunny green and inviting shade. It looked like a good place for a man who had just sold his first graphic novel—*and* its sequel, both for

an amazing amount of money—to sit and eat a chocolate ice cream cone.

When he looked back, the three kids in the baggies
were gone and the woman in the power suit was order-
ing a sundae. One of the two girls behind her had a
peppermint-colored phone clipped to her hip, and the
woman in the power suit had hers screwed into her ear.
Clay thought, as he almost always did on one level of
his mind or another when he saw a variation of this
behavior, that he was watching an act which would once
have been considered almost insufferably rude—yes,
even while engaging in a small bit of commerce with a
total stranger—becoming a part of accepted everyday
behavior.

Put it in Dark Wanderer, *sweetheart,* Sharon said. The
version of her he kept in his mind spoke often and was
bound to have her say. This was true of the real-world
Sharon as well, separation or no separation. Although
not on his cell phone. Clay didn't own one.

The peppermint-colored phone played the opening
notes of that Crazy Frog tune that Johnny loved—was
it called "Axel F"? Clay couldn't remember, perhaps
because he had blocked it out. The girl to whom the
phone belonged snatched it off her hip and said,
"Beth?" She listened, smiled, then said to her compan-
ion, "It's Beth." Now the other girl bent forward and
they both listened, nearly identical pixie haircuts (to
Clay they looked almost like Saturday-morning cartoon
characters, the Powerpuff Girls, maybe) blowing
together in the afternoon breeze.

"Maddy?" said the woman in the power suit at
almost exactly the same time. Her poodle was now sitting contemplatively at the end of its leash (the leash
was red, and dusted with glittery stuff), looking at the

traffic on Boylston Street. Across the way, at the Four Seasons, a doorman in a brown uniform—they always seemed to be brown or blue—was waving, probably for a taxi. A Duck Boat crammed with tourists sailed by, looking high and out of place on dry land, the driver bawling into his loudhailer about something historic. The two girls listening to the peppermint-colored phone looked at each other and smiled at something they were hearing, but still did not giggle.

"Maddy? Can you hear me? *Can you*—"

The woman in the power suit raised the hand holding the leash and plugged a long-nailed finger into her free ear. Clay winced, fearing for her eardrum. He imagined drawing her: the dog on the leash, the power suit, the fashionably short hair . . . and one small trickle of blood from around the finger in her ear. The Duck Boat just exiting the frame and the doorman in the background, those things somehow lending the sketch its verisimilitude. They would; it was just a thing you knew.

"Maddy, you're breaking *up*! I just wanted to tell you I got my hair done at that new . . . my *hair*? . . . *MY* . . ."

The guy in the Mister Softee truck bent down and held out a sundae cup. From it rose a white Alp with chocolate and strawberry sauce coursing down its sides. His beard-stubbly face was impassive. It said he'd seen it all before Clay was sure he had, most of it twice. In the park, someone screamed. Clay looked over his shoulder again, telling himself that had to be a scream of joy. At three o'clock in the afternoon, a sunny afternoon on the Boston Common, it pretty much *had* to be a scream of joy. Right?

The woman said something unintelligible to Maddy and flipped her cell phone closed with a practiced flip of the wrist. She dropped it back into her purse, then just stood there, as if she had forgotten what she was doing or maybe even where she was.

"That's four-fifty," said the Mister Softee guy, still patiently holding out the ice cream sundae. Clay had time to think how fucking *expensive* everything was in the city. Perhaps the woman in the power suit thought so, too—that, at least, was his first surmise—because for a moment more she still did nothing, merely looked at the cup with its mound of ice cream and sliding sauce as if she had never seen such a thing before.

Then there came another cry from the Common, not a human one this time but something between a surprised yelp and a hurt yowl. Clay turned to look and saw the dog that had been trotting with the Frisbee in its mouth. It was a good-sized brown dog, maybe a Labrador, he didn't really know dogs, when he needed to draw one he got a book and copied a picture. A man in a business suit was down on his knees beside this one and had it in a necklock and appeared to be—*surely I'm not seeing what I think I'm seeing,* Clay thought—chewing on its ear. Then the dog howled again and tried to spurt away. The man in the business suit held it firm, and yes, that was the dog's ear in the man's mouth, and as Clay continued to watch, the man tore it off the side of the dog's head. This time the dog uttered an almost human scream, and a number of ducks which had been floating on a nearby pond took flight, squawking.

"*Rast!*" someone cried from behind Clay. It sounded like *rast.* It might have been *rat* or *roast,* but later experience made him lean toward *rast:* not a word at all but merely an inarticulate sound of aggression.

He turned back toward the ice cream truck in time to see Power Suit Woman lunge through the serving window in an effort to grab Mister Softee Guy. She managed to snag the loose folds at the front of his white tunic, but his single startle-step backward was enough to break her hold. Her high heels briefly left the side-walk, and he heard the rasp of cloth and the clink of buttons as the front of her jacket ran first up the little jut of the serving window's counter and then back down. The sundae tumbled from view. Clay saw a smear of ice cream and sauce on Power Suit Woman's left wrist and forearm as her high heels clacked back to the side-walk. She staggered, knees bent. The closed-off, well-bred, out-in-public look on her face—what Clay thought of as your basic on-the-street-no-face look—had been replaced by a convulsive snarl that shrank her eyes to slits and exposed both sets of teeth. Her upper lip had turned completely inside out, revealing a pink velvet lining as intimate as a vulva. Her poodle ran into the street, trailing its red leash with the hand-loop in the end. A black limo came along and ran the poodle down before it got halfway across. Fluff at one moment; guts at the next.

Poor damn thing was probably yapping in doggy heaven before it knew it was dead, Clay thought. He understood in some clinical way he was in shock, but that in no way changed the depth of his amazement. He stood there with his portfolio hanging from one hand and his brown shopping bag hanging from the other and his mouth hanging open.

Somewhere—it sounded like maybe around the cor-ner on Newbury Street—something exploded.

The two girls had exactly the same haircut above their iPod headphones, but the one with the pepper-mint-colored cell phone was blond and her friend was brunette; they were Pixie Light and Pixie Dark. Now

Pixie Light dropped her phone on the sidewalk, where it shattered, and seized Power Suit Woman around the waist. Clay assumed (so far as he was capable of assuming anything in those moments) that she meant to restrain Power Suit Woman either from going after Mister Softee Guy again or from running into the street after her dog. There was even a part of his mind that applauded the girl's presence of mind. Her friend, Pixie Dark, was backing away from the whole deal, small white hands clasped between her breasts, eyes wide.

Clay dropped his own items, one on each side, and stepped forward to help Pixie Light. On the other side of the street—he saw this only in his peripheral vision— a car swerved and bolted across the sidewalk in front of the Four Seasons, causing the doorman to dart out of the way. There were screams from the hotel's forecourt. And before Clay could begin helping Pixie Light with Power Suit Woman, Pixie Light had darted her pretty little face forward with snakelike speed, bared her undoubtedly strong young teeth, and battened on Power Suit Woman's neck. There was an enormous jet of blood. The pixie-girl stuck her face in it, appeared to bathe in it, perhaps even drank from it (Clay was almost sure she did), then shook Power Suit Woman back and forth like a doll. The woman was taller and had to outweigh the girl by at least forty pounds, but the girl shook her hard enough to make the woman's head flop back and forth and send more blood flying. At the same time the girl cocked her own blood-smeared face up to the bright blue October sky and howled in what sounded like triumph.

She's mad, Clay thought. *Totally mad.*

Pixie Dark cried out, "Who are you? *What's happening?*" At the sound of her friend's voice, Pixie Light whipped her bloody head around. Blood dripped from the short dagger-points of hair overhanging her forehead. Eyes like white lamps peered from blood-dappled sockets.

Pixie Dark looked at Clay, her eyes wide. "Who are you?" she repeated . . . and then: "Who am *I*?"

Pixie Light dropped Power Suit Woman, who collapsed to the sidewalk with her chewed-open carotid artery still spurting, then leaped at the girl with whom she had been chummily sharing a phone only a few moments before.

Clay didn't think. If he had thought, Pixie Dark might have had her throat opened like the woman in the power suit. He didn't even look. He simply reached down and to his right, seized the top of the **small treasures** shopping bag, and swung it at the back of Pixie Light's head as she leaped at her erstwhile friend with her outstretched hands making claw-fish against the blue sky. If he missed—

He didn't miss, or even hit the girl a glancing blow. The glass paperweight inside the bag struck the back of Pixie Light's head dead-on, making a muffled *thunk*. Pixie Light dropped her hands, one bloodstained, one still clean, and fell to the sidewalk at her friend's feet like a sack of mail.

"What the *hell*?" Mister Softee Guy cried. His voice was improbably high. Maybe shock had given him that high tenor.

"I don't know," Clay said. His heart was hammering. "Help me quick. This other one's bleeding to death."

From behind them, on Newbury Street, came the unmistakable hollow bang-and-jingle of a car crash, followed by screams. The screams were followed by another explosion, this one louder, concussive, hammering the day. Behind the Mister Softee truck, another car swerved across three lanes of Boylston Street and into the courtyard of the Four Seasons, mowing down a couple of pedestrians and then plowing into the back of the previous car, which had finished with its nose crumpled into the revolving doors. This second crash shoved the first car farther into the revolving doors, bending them askew. Clay couldn't see if anyone was trapped in there—clouds of steam were rising from the first car's breached radiator—but the agonized shrieks from the shadows suggested bad things. Very bad.

Mister Softee Guy, blind on that side, was leaning out his serving window and staring at Clay. "What's going on over there?"

"I don't know. Couple of car wrecks. People hurt. Never mind. Help me, man." He knelt beside Power Suit Woman in the blood and the shattered remnants of Pixie Light's pink cell phone. Power Suit Woman's twitches had now become weak, indeed.

"Smoke from over on Newbury," observed Mister Softee Guy, still not emerging from the relative safety of his ice cream wagon. "Something blew up over there. I mean bigtime. Maybe it's terrorists."

As soon as the word was out of his mouth, Clay was sure he was right. "Help me."

"WHO AM I?" Pixie Dark suddenly screamed.

Clay had forgotten all about her. He looked up in time to see the girl smack herself in the forehead with the heel of her hand, then turn around rapidly three times, standing almost on the toes of her tennies to do it. The sight called up a memory of some poem he'd read in a college lit class—*Weave a circle round him thrice.* Coleridge, wasn't it? She staggered, then ran rapidly down the sidewalk and directly into a lamppost. She made no attempt to avoid it or even put up her hands. She struck it face-first, rebounded, staggered, then went at it again.

"Stop that!" Clay roared. He shot to his feet, started to run toward her, slipped in Power Suit Woman's blood, almost fell, got going again, tripped on Pixie Light, and almost fell again.

Pixie Dark looked around at him. Her nose was broken and gushing blood down her lower face. A vertical contusion was puffing up on her brow, rising like a thunderhead on a summer day. One of her eyes had gone crooked in its socket. She opened her mouth, exposing a ruin of what had probably been expensive orthodontic work, and laughed at him. He never forgot it.

Then she ran away down the sidewalk, screaming.

Behind him, a motor started up and amplified bells began tinkling out the *Sesame Street* theme. Clay turned and saw the Mister Softee truck pulling rapidly away from the curb just as, from the top floor of the hotel across the way, a window shattered in a bright spray of glass. A body hurtled out into the October day. It fell to the sidewalk, where it more or less exploded. More screams from the forecourt. Screams of horror; screams of pain.

"No!" Clay yelled, running alongside the Mister Softee truck. *"No, come back and help me! I need some help here, you sonofabitch!"*

No answer from Mister Softee Guy, who maybe couldn't hear over his amplified music. Clay could remember the words from the days when he'd had no reason not to believe his marriage wouldn't last forever. In those days Johnny watched *Sesame Street* every day, sitting in his little blue chair with his sippy cup clutched in his hands. Something about a sunny day, keepin' the clouds away.

A man in a business suit came running out of the park, roaring wordless sounds at the top of his lungs, his coattails flapping behind him. Clay recognized him by his dogfur goatee. The man ran into Boylston Street. Cars swerved around him, barely missing him. He ran on to the other side, still roaring and waving his hands at the sky. He disappeared into the shadows beneath the canopy of the Four Seasons forecourt and was lost to view, but he must have gotten up to more dickens immediately, because a fresh volley of screams broke out over there.

Clay gave up his chase of the Mister Softee truck and stood with one foot on the sidewalk and the other planted in the gutter, watching as it swerved into the center lane of Boylston Street, still tinkling. He was about to turn back to the unconscious girl and dying woman when another Duck Boat appeared, this one not loafing but roaring at top speed and yawing crazily from port to starboard. Some of the passengers were tumbling back and forth and howling—*pleading*—for the driver to stop. Others simply clung to the metal struts running up the open sides of the ungainly thing as it made its way up Boylston Street against the flow of traffic.

A man in a sweatshirt grabbed the driver from behind, and Clay heard another of those inarticulate cries through the Duck Boat's primitive amplification system as the driver threw the guy off with a mighty backward shrug. Not *"Rast!"* this time but something more guttural, something that sounded like *"Gluh!"* Then the Duck Boat driver saw the Mister Softee truck—Clay was sure of it—and changed course, aiming for it.

"Oh God please no!" a woman sitting near the front of the tourist craft cried, and as it closed in on the tinkling

ice cream truck, which was approximately one-sixth its size, Clay had a clear memory of watching the victory parade on TV the year the Red Sox won the World Series. The team rode in a slow-moving procession of these same Duck Boats, waving to the delirious multitudes as a cold autumn drizzle fell.

"God please no!" the woman shrieked again, and from beside Clay a man said, almost mildly: "Jesus Christ."

The Duck Boat hit the ice cream truck broadside and flipped it like a child's toy. It landed on its side with its own amplification system still tinkling out the *Sesame Street* theme music and went skidding back toward the Common, shooting up friction-generated bursts of sparks. Two women who had been watching dashed to get out of the way, holding hands, and just made it. The Mister Softee truck bounced onto the sidewalk, went briefly airborne, then hit the wrought-iron fence surrounding the park and came to rest. The music hiccuped twice, then stopped.

The lunatic driving the Duck Boat had, meanwhile, lost whatever marginal control he might have had over his vehicle. It looped back across Boylston Street with its freight of terrified, screaming passengers clinging to the open sides, mounted the sidewalk across and about fifty yards down from the point where the Mister Softee truck had tinkled its last, and ran into the low brick retaining wall below the display window of a tony furniture shop called Citylights. There was a vast unmusical crash as the window shattered. The Duck Boat's wide rear end (*Harbor Mistress* was written on it in pink script) rose perhaps five feet in the air. Momentum wanted the great waddling thing to go end-over-end; mass would not allow. It settled back to the sidewalk with its snout poked among the scattered sofas and expensive living room chairs, but not before at least a dozen people had gone shooting forward, out of the Duck Boat and out of sight.

Inside Citylights, a burglar alarm began to clang.

"Jesus Christ," said the mild voice from Clay's right elbow a second time. He turned that way and saw a short man with thinning dark hair, a tiny dark mustache, and gold-rimmed spectacles. "What's going on?"

"I don't know," Clay said. Talking was hard. Very. He found himself almost having to push words out. He supposed it was shock. Across the street, people were running away, some from the Four Seasons, some from the crashed Duck Boat. As he watched, a Duck Boat run-awayer collided with a Four Seasons escapee and they both went crashing to the sidewalk. There was time to wonder if he'd gone insane and was hallucinating all this in a madhouse somewhere. Juniper Hill in Augusta, maybe, between Thorazine shots. "The guy in the ice cream truck said maybe terrorists."

"I don't see any men with guns," said the short man with the mustache. "No guys with bombs strapped to their backs, either."

Neither did Clay, but he *did* see his little **small treasures** shopping bag and his portfolio sitting on the sidewalk, and he saw that the blood from Power Suit Woman's opened throat—*ye gods,* he thought, *all that blood*—had almost reached the portfolio. All but a dozen or so of his drawings for *Dark Wanderer* were in there, and it was the drawings his mind seized on. He started back that way at a speed-walk, and the short man kept pace. When a second burglar alarm (*some* kind of alarm, anyway) went off in the hotel, joining its hoarse bray to the clang of the Citylights alarm, the little guy jumped.

"It's the hotel," Clay said.

"I know, it's just that . . . oh my *God*." He'd seen Power Suit Woman, now lying in a lake of the magic stuff that had been running all her bells and whistles—what? Four minutes ago? Only two?

"She's dead," Clay told him. "At least I'm pretty sure she is. That girl . . ." He pointed at Pixie Light. "She did it. With her teeth."

"You're joking."

"I wish I was."

From somewhere up Boylston Street there was another explosion. Both men cringed. Clay realized he could now smell smoke. He picked up his **small treasures** bag and his portfolio and moved them both away from the spreading blood. "These are mine," he said, wondering why he felt the need to explain.

The little guy, who was wearing a tweed suit—quite dapper, Clay thought—was still staring, horrified, at the crumpled body of the woman who had stopped for a sundae and lost first her dog and then her life. Behind them, three young men pelted past on the sidewalk, laughing and hurrahing. Two had Red Sox caps turned around backward. One was carrying a carton clutched against his chest. It had the word **panasonic** printed in blue on the side. This one stepped in Power Suit Woman's spreading blood with his right sneaker and left a fading one-foot trail behind him as he and his mates ran on toward the east end of the Common and Chinatown beyond.

3

Clay dropped to one knee and used the hand not clutching his portfolio (he was even more afraid of losing it after seeing the sprinting kid with the **panasonic** carton) to pick up Pixie Light's wrist. He got a pulse at once. It was slow but strong and regular. He felt great relief. No matter what she'd done, she was just a kid. He didn't want to think he had bludgeoned her to death with his wife's gift paperweight.

"Look out, look out!" the little guy with the mustache almost sang. Clay had no time to look out. Luckily, this call wasn't even close. The vehicle—one of those big OPEC-friendly SUVs—veered off Boylston and into the park at least twenty yards from where he knelt, taking a snarl of the wrought-iron fence in front of it and coming to rest bumper-deep in the duck-pond.

The door opened and a young man floundered out, yelling gibberish at the sky. He fell to his knees in the water, scooped some of it into his mouth with both hands (Clay had a passing thought of all the ducks that had happily shat in that pond over the years), then struggled to his feet and waded to the far side. He disappeared into a grove of trees, still waving his hands and bellowing his nonsense sermon.

"We need to get help for this girl," Clay said to the man with the mustache. "She's unconscious but a long way from dead."

"What we need to *do* is get off the street before we get run over," said the man with the mustache, and as if to prove this point, a taxi collided with a stretch limo not far from the wrecked Duck Boat. The limo had been going the wrong way but the taxi got the worst of it; as Clay watched from where he still knelt on the sidewalk, the taxi's driver flew through his suddenly glassless windshield and landed in the street, holding up a bloody arm and screaming.

The man with the mustache was right, of course. Such rationality as Clay could muster—only a little managed to find its way through the blanket of shock that muffled his thinking—suggested that by far the wisest course of action would be to get the hell away from Boylston Street and under cover. If this was an act of terrorism, it was like none he had ever seen or read about. What he—*they*—should do was get down and stay down until the situation clarified. That would probably entail finding a television. But he didn't want to leave this unconscious girl lying on a street that had suddenly become a madhouse. Every instinct of his mostly kind—and certainly civilized—heart cried out against it.

"You go on," he told the little man with the mustache. He said it with immense reluctance. He didn't know the little man from Adam, but at least he wasn't spouting gibberish and throwing his hands in the air. Or going for Clay's throat with his teeth bared. "Get inside somewhere. I'll . . ." He didn't know how to finish.

"You'll what?" the man with the mustache asked, then hunched his shoulders and winced as something else exploded. That one came from directly behind the hotel, it sounded like, and now black smoke began to rise over there, staining the blue sky before it got high enough for the wind to pull away.

"I'll call a cop," Clay said, suddenly inspired. "She's got a cell phone." He cocked his thumb at Power Suit Woman, now lying dead in a pool of her own blood. "She was using it before . . . you know, just before the shit . . ."

He trailed off, replaying exactly what *had* happened just before the shit hit the fan. He found his eyes wandering from the dead woman to the unconscious girl and then on to the shards of the unconscious girl's peppermint-colored cell phone.

Warbling sirens of two distinctly different pitches rose in the air. Clay supposed one pitch belonged to police cars, the other to fire trucks. He supposed you could tell the difference if you lived in this city, but he didn't, he lived in Kent Pond, Maine, and he wished with all his heart that he were there right now.

What happened just before the shit hit the fan was that Power Suit Woman had called her friend Maddy to tell her she'd gotten her hair done, and one of Pixie Light's friends had called *her*. Pixie Dark had listened in to this latter call. After that all three of them had gone crazy.

You're not thinking—

From behind them, to the east, came the biggest explosion yet: a terrific shotgun-blast of sound. Clay leaped to his feet. He and the little man in the tweed suit looked wildly at each other, then toward China-town and Boston's North End. They couldn't see what had exploded, but now a much larger, darker plume of smoke was rising above the buildings on that horizon.

While they were looking at it, a Boston PD radio-car and a hook-and-ladder fire truck pulled up in front of the Four Seasons across the street. Clay glanced that way in time to see a second jumper set sail from the top story of the hotel, followed by another pair from the roof. To Clay it looked as if the two coming from the roof were actually brawling with each other on the way down.

"Jesus Mary and Joseph NO!" a woman screamed, her voice breaking. *"Oh NO, no MORE, no MORE!"*

The first of the suicidal trio hit the rear of the police car, splattering the trunk with hair and gore, shattering the back window. The other two hit the hook and lad-der as firemen dressed in bright yellow coats scattered like improbable birds.

"NO!" the woman shrieked. *"No MORE! No MORE! Dear GOD, no MORE!"*

But here came a woman from the fifth or sixth floor, tumbling like a crazy acrobat, striking a policeman who was peering up and surely killing him even as she killed herself.

From the north there came another of those great roaring explosions—the sound of the devil firing a shotgun in hell—and once again Clay looked at the little man, who was looking anxiously back up at him. More smoke was rising in the sky, and in spite of the brisk breeze, the blue over there was almost blotted out.

"They're using planes again," the little man said. "The dirty bastards are using planes again."

As if to underline the idea, a third monstrous explosion came rolling to them from the city's northeast.

"But . . . that's Logan over there." Clay was once again finding it hard to talk, and even harder to think. All he really seemed to have in his mind was some sort of half-baked joke: *Did you hear the one about the* [insert your favorite ethnic group here] *terrorists who decided to bring America to its knees by blowing up the airport?*

"So?" the little man asked, almost truculently.

"So why not the Hancock Building? Or the Pru?"

The little man's shoulders slumped. "I don't know. I only know I want to get off this street."

As if to emphasize his point, half a dozen more young people sprinted past them. Boston was a *city* of young people, Clay had noticed—all those colleges. These six, three men and three women, were running lootless, at least, and they most assuredly weren't laughing. As they ran, one of the young men pulled out his cell phone and stuck it to his ear.

Clay glanced across the street and saw that a second

black-and-white unit had pulled up behind the first. No
need to use Power Suit Woman's cell phone after all
(which was good, since he'd decided he really didn't
want to do that). He could just walk across the street
and talk to them . . . except he wasn't sure that he
dared to cross Boylston Street just now. Even if he did,
would they come over *here* to look at one unconscious
girl when they had God knew how many casualties over
there? And as he watched, the firemen began piling back
on board their hook-and-ladder unit; it looked like they
were heading someplace else. Over to Logan Airport,
quite likely, or—

"Oh my God-Jesus, watch out for this one," said the
little man with the mustache, speaking in a low, tight
voice. He was looking west along Boylston, back
toward downtown, in the direction Clay had been coming from when his major object in life had been reaching Sharon on the phone. He'd even known how he was
going to start: *Good news, hon—no matter how it comes out
between us, there'll always be shoes for the kid.* In his head it
had sounded light and funny—like the old days.

There was nothing funny about this. Coming
toward them—not running but walking in long, flat-
footed strides—was a man of about fifty, wearing suit
pants and the remains of a shirt and tie. The pants
were gray. It was impossible to tell what color the shirt
and tie had been, because both were now shredded and
stained with blood. In his right hand the man held
what looked like a butcher knife with an eighteen-inch
blade. Clay actually believed he had seen this knife, in
the window of a shop called Soul Kitchen, on his walk
back from his meeting at the Copley Square Hotel. The
row of knives in the window (**SWEDISH STEEL!** the little
engraved card in front of them proclaimed) had shone

in the cunning glow of hidden downlighters, but this blade had done a good deal of work since its liberation—or a bad deal of it—and was now dull with blood.

The man in the tattered shirt swung the knife as he closed in on them with his flat-footed strides, the blade cutting short up-and-down arcs in the air. He broke the pattern only once, to slash at himself. A fresh rill of blood ran through a new rip in his tattered shirt. The remains of his tie flapped. And as he closed the distance he hectored them like a backwoods preacher speaking in tongues at the moment of some divine godhead revelation.

"*Eyelah!*" he cried. "*Eeelah-eyelah-a-babbalah naz! A-babbalah* why? *A-bunnaloo* coy? *Kazzalah! Kazzalah-*CAN! *Fie!* SHY-*fie!*" And now he brought the knife back to his right hip and then beyond it, and Clay, whose visual sense was overdeveloped, at once saw the sweeping stroke that would follow. The gutting stroke, made even as he continued his nuthouse march to nowhere through the October afternoon in those flat-footed declamatory strides.

"*Look out!*" the little guy with the mustache screamed, but *he* wasn't looking out, not the little guy with the mustache; the little guy with the mustache, the first *normal* person with whom Clay Riddell had spoken since this craziness began—who had, in fact, spoken to *him,* which had probably taken some courage, under the circumstances—was frozen in place, his eyes bigger than ever behind the lenses of his gold-rimmed spectacles. And was the crazy guy going for him because of the two men, the one with the mustache was smaller and looked like easier prey? If so, maybe Mr. Speaking-in-Tongues wasn't *completely* crazy, and suddenly Clay was mad as well as scared, mad the way he might have been if he'd looked through a schoolyard fence and seen a bully getting ready to tune up on a smaller, younger kid.

"LOOK OUT!" the little man with the mustache almost wailed, still not moving as his death swept toward him, death liberated from a shop called Soul Kitchen where Diner's Club and Visa were no doubt accepted, along with Your Personal Check If Accompanied By Bank Card.

Clay didn't think. He simply picked up his portfolio again by its double handle and stuck it between the oncoming knife and his new acquaintance in the tweed suit. The blade went all the way through with a hollow *thuck,* but the tip stopped four inches short of the little man's belly. The little man finally came to his senses and cringed aside, toward the Common, shrieking for help at the top of his lungs.

The man in the shredded shirt and tie—he was getting a bit jowly in the cheek and heavy in the neck, as if his personal equation of good meals and good exercise had stopped balancing about two years ago—abruptly ceased his nonsense peroration. His face took on a look of vacuous perplexity that stopped short of surprise, let alone amazement.

What Clay felt was a species of dismal outrage. That blade had gone through all of his *Dark Wanderer* pictures (to him they were always pictures, never drawings or illustrations), and it seemed to him that the *thuck* sound might as well have been the blade penetrating a special chamber of his heart. That was stupid when he had repros of everything, including the four color splash-pages, but it didn't change how he felt. The madman's blade had skewered Sorcerer John (named after his own son, of course), the Wizard Flak, Frank and the Posse Boys, Sleepy Gene, Poison Sally, Lily Astolet, Blue Witch, and of course Ray Damon, the Dark Wanderer himself. His own fantastic creatures, living in the cave of his imagination and poised to set him free from the drudgery of teaching art in a dozen rural Maine schools, driving thousands of miles a month and practically living out of his car.

He could swear he had heard them moan when the madman's Swedish blade pierced them where they slept in their innocency.

Furious, not caring about the blade (at least for the moment), he drove the man in the shredded shirt rapidly backward, using the portfolio as a kind of shield, growing angrier as it bent into a wide V-shape around the knife-blade.

"Blet!" the lunatic hollered, and tried to pull his blade back. It was caught too firmly for him to do so. *"Blet ky-yam doe-ram kazzalah a-babbalah!"*

"I'll a-babbalah *your* a-kazzalah, you fuck!" Clay shouted, and planted his left foot behind the lunatic's backpedaling legs. It would occur to him later that the body knows how to fight when it has to. That it's a secret the body keeps, just as it does the secrets of how to run or jump a creek or throw a fuck or—quite likely—die when there's no other choice. That under conditions of extreme stress it simply takes over and does what needs doing while the brain stands off to one side, unable to do anything but whistle and tap its foot and look up at the sky. Or contemplate the sound a knife makes going through the portfolio your wife gave you for your twenty-eighth birthday, for that matter.

The lunatic tripped over Clay's foot just as Clay's wise body meant him to do and fell to the sidewalk on his back. Clay stood over him, panting, with the portfolio still held in both hands like a shield bent in battle. The butcher knife still stuck out of it, handle from one side, blade from the other.

The lunatic tried to get up. Clay's new friend scurried forward and kicked him in the neck, quite hard. The little fellow was weeping loudly, the tears gushing down his cheeks and fogging the lenses of his spectacles. The lunatic fell back on the sidewalk with his tongue sticking out of his mouth. Around it he made choking sounds that sounded to Clay like his former speaking-in-tongues babble.

"He tried to kill us!" the little man wept. "He tried to *kill* us!"

"Yes, yes," Clay said. He was aware that he had once said *yes, yes* to Johnny in exactly the same way back when they'd still called him Johnny-Gee and he'd come to them up the front walk with his scraped shins or elbows, wailing *I got BLOOD!*

The man on the sidewalk (who had plenty of blood) was on his elbows, trying to get up again. Clay did the honors this time, kicking one of the guy's elbows out from under him and putting him back down on the pavement. This kicking seemed like a stopgap solution at best, and a messy one. Clay grabbed the handle of the knife, winced at the slimy feel of half-jellied blood on the handle—it was like rubbing a palm through cold bacon-grease—and pulled. The knife came a little bit, then either stopped or his hand slipped. He fancied he heard his characters murmuring unhappily from the darkness of the portfolio, and he made a painful noise himself. He couldn't help it. And he couldn't help wondering what he meant to do with the knife if he got it out. Stab the lunatic to death with it? He thought he could have done that in the heat of the moment, but probably not now.

"What's wrong?" the little man asked in a watery voice. Clay, even in his own distress, couldn't help being touched by the concern he heard there. "Did he get you? You had him blocked out for a few seconds and I couldn't see. Did he get you? Are you cut?"

"No," Clay said. "I'm all r—"

There was another gigantic explosion from the north, almost surely from Logan Airport on the other side of Boston Harbor. Both of them hunched their shoulders and winced.

The lunatic took the opportunity to sit up and was scrambling to his feet when the little man in the tweed suit administered a clumsy but effective sideways kick, planting a shoe squarely in the middle of the lunatic's shredded tie and knocking him back down. The lunatic roared and snatched at the little man's foot. He would have pulled the little guy over, then perhaps into a crushing embrace, had Clay not seized his new acquaintance by the shoulder and pulled him away.

"He's got my shoe!" the little man yelped. Behind them, two more cars crashed. There were more screams, more alarms. Car alarms, fire alarms, hearty clanging burglar alarms. Sirens whooped in the distance. *"Bastard got my sh—"*

Suddenly a policeman was there. One of the responders from across the street, Clay assumed, and as the policeman dropped to one blue knee beside the babbling lunatic, Clay felt something very much like love for the cop. That he'd take the time to come over here! That he'd even noticed!

"You want to be careful of him," the little man said nervously. "He's—"

"I know what he is," the cop replied, and Clay saw the cop had his service automatic in his hand. He had no idea if the cop had drawn it after kneeling or if he'd had it out the whole time. Clay had been too busy being grateful to notice.

The cop looked at the lunatic. Leaned close to the lunatic. Almost seemed to *offer* himself to the lunatic. "Hey, buddy, how ya doin?" he murmured. "I mean, what the haps?"

The lunatic lunged at the cop and put his hands on the cop's throat. The instant he did this, the cop slipped the muzzle of his gun into the hollow of the lunatic's temple and pulled the trigger. A great spray of blood leaped through the graying hair on the opposite side of the lunatic's head and he fell back to the sidewalk, throwing both arms out melodramatically: *Look, Ma, I'm dead.*

Clay looked at the little man with the mustache and the little man with the mustache looked at him. Then they looked back at the cop, who had holstered his weapon and was taking a leather case from the breast pocket of his uniform shirt. Clay was glad to see that the hand he used to do this was shaking a little. He was now frightened of the cop, but would have been more frightened still if the cop's hands had been steady. And what had just happened was no isolated case. The gunshot seemed to have done something to Clay's hearing, cleared a circuit in it or something. Now he could hear other gunshots, isolated cracks punctuating the escalating cacophony of the day.

The cop took a card—Clay thought it was a business card—from the slim leather case, then put the case back in his breast pocket. He held the card between the first two fingers of his left hand while his right hand once more dropped to the butt of his service weapon. Near his highly polished shoes, blood from the lunatic's shattered head was pooling on the sidewalk. Close by, Power Suit Woman lay in another pool of blood, which was now starting to congeal and turn a darker shade of red.

"What's your name, sir?" the cop asked Clay.

"Clayton Riddell."

"Can you tell me who the president is?"

Clay told him.

"Sir, can you tell me today's date?"

"It's the first of October. Do you know what's—"

The cop looked at the little man with the mustache. "Your name?"

"I'm Thomas McCourt, 140 Salem Street, Malden. I—"

"Can you name the man who ran against the president in the last election?"

Tom McCourt did so.

"Who is Brad Pitt married to?"

McCourt threw up his hands. "How should *I* know? Some movie star, I think."

"Okay." The cop handed Clay the card he'd been holding between his fingers. "I'm Officer Ulrich Ashland. This is my card. You may be called on to testify about what just happened here, gentlemen. What happened was you needed assistance, I rendered it, I was attacked, I responded."

"You wanted to kill him," Clay said.

"Yes, sir, we're putting as many of them out of their misery as fast as we can," Officer Ashland agreed. "And if you tell any court or board of inquiry that I said that, I'll deny it. But it has to be done. These people are popping up everywhere. Some only commit suicide. Many others attack." He hesitated, then added: "So far as we can tell, *all* the others attack." As if to underline this, there was another gunshot from across the street, a pause, then three more, in rapid succession, from the shadowed forecourt of the Four Seasons Hotel, which was now a tangle of broken glass, broken bodies, crashed vehicles, and spilled blood. "It's like the fucking *Night of the Living Dead*." Officer Ulrich Ashland started back toward Boylston Street with his hand still on the butt of his gun. "Except these people aren't dead. Unless we help them, that is."

"Rick!" It was a cop on the other side of the street, calling urgently. "Rick, we gotta go to Logan! All units! Get over here!"

Officer Ashland checked for traffic, but there was none. Except for the wrecks, Boylston Street was momentarily deserted. From the surrounding area, however, came the sound of more explosions and automotive crashes. The smell of smoke was getting stronger. He started across the street, got halfway, then turned back. "Get inside somewhere," he said. "Get under cover. You've been lucky once. You may not be lucky again."

"Officer Ashland," Clay said. "Your guys don't use cell phones, do you?"

Ashland regarded him from the center of Boylston Street—not, in Clay's opinion, a safe place to be. He was thinking of the rogue Duck Boat. "No, sir," he said. "We have radios in our cars. And these." He patted the radio in his belt, hung opposite his holster. Clay, a comic-book fiend since he could read, thought briefly of Batman's marvelous utility belt.

"Don't use them," Clay said. "Tell the others. *Don't use the cell phones.*"

"Why do you say that?"

"Because *they* were." He pointed to the dead woman and the unconscious girl. "Just before they went crazy. And I'll bet you anything that the guy with the knife—"

"*Rick!*" the cop on the other side shouted again. "*Hurry the fuck up!*"

"Get under cover," Officer Ashland repeated, and trotted to the Four Seasons side of the street. Clay wished he could have repeated the thing about the cell phones, but on the whole he was just glad to see the cop out of harm's way. Not that he believed anyone in Boston really was, not this afternoon.

4

"What are you doing?" Clay asked Tom McCourt. "Don't touch him, he might be, I don't know, contagious."

"I'm not going to touch him," Tom said, "but I need my shoe."

The shoe, lying near the splayed fingers of the lunatic's left hand, was at least away from the exit-spray of blood. Tom hooked his fingers delicately into the back and pulled it to him. Then he sat down on the curb of Boylston Street—right where the Mister Softee truck had been parked in what now seemed to Clay like another lifetime—and slipped his foot into it. "The laces are broken," he said. "That damn nutball broke the laces." And he started crying again.

"Do the best you can," Clay said. He began working the butcher knife out of the portfolio. It had been slammed through with tremendous force, and he found he had to wiggle it up and down to free it. It came out reluctantly, in a series of jerks, and with ugly scraping sounds that made him want to cringe. He kept wondering who inside had gotten the worst of it. That was stu-

pid, nothing but shock-think, but he couldn't help it.
"Can't you tie it down close to the bottom?"

"Yeah, I think s—"

Clay had been hearing a mechanical mosquito whine
that now grew to an approaching drone. Tom craned up
from his place on the curb. Clay turned around. The little caravan of BPD cars pulling away from the Four Seasons halted in front of Citylights and the crashed Duck
Boat with their gumballs flashing. Cops leaned out the
windows as a private plane—something midsize, maybe
a Cessna or the kind they called a Twin Bonanza, Clay
didn't really know planes—came cruising slowly over
the buildings between Boston Harbor and the Boston
Common, dropping fast. The plane banked drunkenly
over the park, its lower wing almost brushing the top of
one autumn-bright tree, then settled into the canyon of
Charles Street, as if the pilot had decided that was a
runway. Then, less than twenty feet above the ground,
it tilted left and the wing on that side struck the façade
of a gray stone building, maybe a bank, on the corner of
Charles and Beacon. Any sense that the plane was moving slowly, almost gliding, departed in that instant. It
spun around on the caught wing as savagely as a teth-
erball nearing the end of its rope, slammed into the red-
brick building standing next to the bank, and
disappeared in bright petals of red-orange fire. The
shockwave hammered across the park. Ducks took wing
before it.

Clay looked down and saw he was holding the
butcher knife in his hand. He had pulled it free while
he and Tom McCourt were watching the plane crash.
He wiped it first one way and then the other on the
front of his shirt, taking pains not to cut himself (now
his hands were shaking). Then he slipped it—very

carefully—into his belt, all the way down to the handle. As he did this, one of his early comic-book efforts occurred to him . . . a bit of juvenilia, actually.

"Joxer the Pirate stands here at your service, my pretty one," he murmured.

"What?" Tom asked. He was now beside Clay, staring at the boiling inferno of the airplane on the far side of Boston Common. Only the tail stuck out of the fire. On it Clay could read the number **LN6409B**. Above it was what looked like some sports team's logo.

Then that was gone, too.

He could feel the first waves of heat begin to pump gently against his face.

"Nothing," he told the little man in the tweed suit. "Leave us boogie."

"Huh?"

"Let's get out of here."

"Oh. Okay."

Clay started to walk along the southern side of the Common, in the direction he'd been heading at three o'clock, eighteen minutes and an eternity ago. Tom McCourt hurried to keep up. He really was a *very* short man. "Tell me," he said, "do you often talk nonsense?"

"Sure," Clay said. "Just ask my wife."

5

"Where are we going?" Tom asked. "I was headed for the T." He pointed to a green-painted kiosk about a block ahead. A small crowd of people were milling there. "Now I'm not sure being underground is such a hot idea."

"Me, either," Clay said. "I've got a room at a place called the Atlantic Avenue Inn, about five blocks further up."

Tom brightened. "I think I know it. On Louden, actually, just *off* Atlantic."

"Right. Let's go there. We can check the TV. And I want to call my wife."

"On the room phone."

"The room phone, check. I don't even *have* a cell phone."

"I have one, but I left it home. It's broken. Rafe—my cat—knocked it off the counter. I was meaning to buy a new one this very day, but . . . listen. Mr. Rid-dell—"

"Clay."

"Clay, then. Are you sure the phone in your room will be safe?"

Clay stopped. He hadn't even considered this idea. But if the landlines weren't okay, what *would* be? He was about to say this to Tom when a sudden brawl broke out at the T station up ahead. There were cries of panic, screams, and more of that wild babbling—he recognized it for what it was now, the signature scribble of madness. The little knot of people that had been milling around the gray stone pillbox and the steps going belowground broke up. A few of them ran into the street, two with their arms around each other, snatching looks back over their shoulders as they went. More—most—ran into the park, all in different directions, which sort of broke Clay's heart. He felt better somehow about the two with their arms around each other.

Still at the T station and on their feet were two men and two women. Clay was pretty sure it was they who had emerged from the station and driven off the rest. As Clay and Tom stood watching from half a block away, these remaining four fell to fighting with each other. This brawl had the hysterical, killing viciousness he had already seen, but no discernible pattern. It wasn't three against one, or two against two, and it certainly wasn't the boys against the girls; in fact, one of the "girls" was a woman who looked to be in her middle sixties, with a stocky body and a no-nonsense haircut that made Clay think of several women teachers he'd known who were nearing retirement.

They fought with feet and fists and nails and teeth, grunting and shouting and circling the bodies of maybe half a dozen people who had already been knocked unconscious, or perhaps killed. One of the men stumbled over an outstretched leg and went to his knees. The younger of the two women dropped on top of him. The man on his knees swept something up from the pave- ment at the head of the stairs—Clay saw with no sur- prise whatever that it was a cell phone—and slammed it into the side of the woman's face. The cell phone shat- tered, tearing the woman's cheek open and showering a freshet of blood onto the shoulder of her light jacket, but her scream was of rage rather than pain. She grabbed the kneeling man's ears like a pair of jughandles, dropped her own knees into his lap, and shoved him backwards into the gloom of the T's stairwell. They went out of sight locked together and thrashing like cats in heat.

"Come on," Tom murmured, twitching Clay's shirt with an odd delicacy. "Come on. Other side of the street. Come on."

Clay allowed himself to be led across Boylston Street. He assumed that either Tom McCourt was watching where they were going or he was lucky, because they got to the other side okay. They stopped again in front of Colonial Books (Best of the Old, Best of the New), watching as the unlikely victor of the T station battle went striding into the park in the direction of the burning plane, with blood dripping onto her collar from the ends of her zero-tolerance gray hair. Clay wasn't a bit surprised that the last one standing had turned out to be the lady who looked like a librarian or Latin teacher a year or two away from a gold watch. He had taught with his share of such ladies, and the ones who made it to that age were, more often than not, next door to indestructible.

He opened his mouth to say something like this to Tom—in his mind it sounded quite witty—and what came out was a watery croak. His vision had come over shimmery, too. Apparently Tom McCourt, the little man in the tweed suit, wasn't the only one having trouble with his waterworks. Clay swiped an arm across his eyes, tried again to talk, and managed no more than another of those watery croaks.

"That's okay," Tom said. "Better let it come."

And so, standing there in front of a shop window filled with old books surrounding a Royal typewriter hailing from long before the era of cellular communications, Clay did. He cried for Power Suit Woman, for Pixie Light and Pixie Dark, and he cried for himself, because Boston was not his home, and home had never seemed so far.

6

Above the Common Boylston Street narrowed and became so choked with cars—both those wrecked and those plain abandoned—that they no longer had to worry about kamikaze limos or rogue Duck Boats. Which was a relief. From all around them the city banged and crashed like New Year's Eve in hell. There was plenty of noise close by, as well—car alarms and burglar alarms, mostly—but the street itself was for the moment eerily deserted. *Get under cover,* Officer Ulrich Ashland had said. *You've been lucky once. You may not be lucky again.*

But, two blocks east of Colonial Books and still a block from Clay's not-quite-fleabag hotel, they *were* lucky again. Another lunatic, this one a young man of perhaps twenty-five with muscles that looked tuned by Nautilus and Cybex, bolted from an alley just in front of them and went dashing across the street, hurdling the locked bumpers of two cars, foaming out an unceasing lava-flow of that nonsense-talk as he went. He held a car aerial in each hand and stabbed them rapidly back and forth in the air like daggers as he cruised his lethal course. He was naked except for a pair of what looked like brand-new Nikes with bright red swooshes. His cock swung from side to side like the pendulum of a grandfather clock on speed. He hit the far sidewalk and sidewheeled west, back toward the Common, his butt clenching and unclenching in fantastic rhythm.

Tom McCourt clutched Clay's arm, and hard, until this latest lunatic was gone, then slowly relaxed his grip. "If he'd seen us—" he began.

"Yeah, but he didn't," Clay said. He felt suddenly, absurdly happy. He knew that the feeling would pass, but for the moment he was delighted to ride it. He felt like a man who has successfully drawn to an inside straight with the biggest pot of the night lying on the table in front of him.

"I pity who he *does* see," Tom said.

"I pity who sees *him,*" Clay said. "Come on."

7

The doors of the Atlantic Avenue Inn were locked.

Clay was so surprised that for a moment he could

only stand there, trying to turn the knob and feeling it slip through his fingers, trying to get the idea through his head: locked. The doors of his hotel, locked against him.

Tom stepped up beside him, leaned his forehead against the glass to cut the glare, and peered in. From the north—from Logan, surely—came another of those monster explosions, and this time Clay only twitched. He didn't think Tom McCourt reacted at all. Tom was too absorbed in what he was seeing.

"Dead guy on the floor," he announced at last. "Wearing a uniform, but he really looks too old to be a bellhop."

"I don't want anyone to carry my fucking luggage," Clay said. "I just want to go up to my room."

Tom made an odd little snorting sound. Clay thought maybe the little guy was starting to cry again, then realized that sound was smothered laughter.

The double doors had **ATLANTIC AVENUE INN** printed on one glass panel and a blatant lie— **BOSTON'S FINEST ADDRESS**—printed on the other. Tom slapped the flat of his hand on the glass of the lefthand panel, between **BOSTON'S FINEST ADDRESS** and a row of credit card decals.

Now Clay was peering in, too. The lobby wasn't very big. On the left was the reception desk. On the right was a pair of elevators. On the floor was a turkey-red rug. The old guy in the uniform lay on this, facedown, with one foot up on a couch and a framed Currier & Ives sailing-ship print on his ass.

Clay's good feelings left in a rush, and when Tom began to hammer on the glass instead of just slap, he put his hand over Tom's fist. "Don't bother," he said. "They're not going to let us in, even if they're alive and sane." He thought about that and nodded. "*Especially* if they're sane."

Tom looked at him wonderingly. "You don't get it, do you?"

"Huh? Get what?"

"Things have changed. They can't keep us out." He pushed Clay's hand off his own, but instead of hammering, he put his forehead against the glass again and shouted. Clay thought he had a pretty good shouting voice on him for a little guy. *"Hey! Hey, in there!"*

A pause. In the lobby nothing changed. The old bellman went on being dead with a picture on his ass.

"Hey, if you're in there, you better open the door! The man I'm with is a paying guest of the hotel and I'm his guest! Open up or I'm going to grab a curbstone and break the glass! You hear me?"

"A *curb*stone?" Clay said. He started to laugh. "Did you say *curb*stone? Jolly *good*." He laughed harder. He couldn't help it. Then movement to his left caught his eye. He looked around and saw a teenage girl standing a little way farther up the street. She was looking at them out of haggard blue disaster-victim eyes. She was wearing a white dress, and there was a vast bib of blood on the front of it. More blood was crusted beneath her nose, on her lips and chin. Other than the bloody nose she didn't look hurt, and she didn't look crazy at all, just shocked. Shocked almost to death.

"Are you all right?" Clay asked. He took a step toward her and she took a corresponding step back. Under the circumstances, he couldn't blame her. He stopped but held a hand up to her like a traffic cop: *Stay put.*

Tom glanced around briefly, then began to hammer on the door again, this time hard enough to rattle the glass in its old wooden frame and make his reflection shiver. *"Last chance, then we're coming in!"*

Clay turned and opened his mouth to tell him that masterful shit wasn't going to cut it, not today, and then a bald head rose slowly from behind the reception desk. It was like watching a periscope surface. Clay recognized that head even before it got to the face; it belonged to the clerk who'd checked him in yesterday and stamped a validation on his parking-lot ticket for the lot a block over, the same clerk who'd given him directions to the Copley Square Hotel this morning.

For a moment he still lingered behind the desk, and Clay held up his room key with the green plastic Atlantic Avenue Inn fob hanging down. Then he also held up his portfolio, thinking the desk clerk might recognize it.

Maybe he did. More likely he just decided he had no choice. In either case, he used the pass-through at the end of the desk and crossed quickly to the door, detouring around the body. Clay Riddell believed he might be witnessing the first reluctant scurry he had ever seen in his life. When the desk clerk reached the other side of the door, he looked from Clay to Tom and then back to Clay again. Although he did not appear particularly reassured by what he saw, he produced a ring of keys from one pocket, flicked rapidly through them, found one, and used it on his side of the door. When Tom reached for the handle, the bald clerk held his hand up much as Clay had held his up to the bloodstained girl behind them. The clerk found a second key, used this one in another lock, and opened the door.

"Come in," he said. "Hurry." Then he saw the girl, lingering at a little distance and watching. *"Not her."*

"Yes, her," Clay said. "Come on, honey." But she wouldn't, and when Clay took a step toward her, she whirled and took off running, the skirt of her dress flying out behind her.

8

"She could die out there," Clay said.

"Not my problem," the desk clerk said. "Are you coming in or not, Mr. Riddle?" He had a Boston accent, not the blue-collar-Southie kind Clay was most familiar with from Maine, where it seemed that every third person you met was a Massachusetts expat, but the fussy I-wish-I-were-British one.

"It's Riddell." He was coming in all right, no way this guy was going to keep him out now that the door was open, but he lingered a moment longer on the sidewalk, looking after the girl.

"Go on," Tom said quietly. "Nothing to be done."

And he was right. Nothing to be done. That was the exact hell of it. He followed Tom in, and the desk clerk once more double-locked the doors of the Atlantic Avenue Inn behind them, as if that were all it would take to keep them from the chaos of the streets.

9

"That was Franklin," said the desk clerk as he led the way around the uniformed man lying facedown on the floor.

He looks too old to be a bellhop, Tom had said, peering in through the window, and Clay thought he certainly did. He was a small man, with a lot of luxuriant white hair. Unfortunately for him, the head on which it was probably still growing (hair and nails were slow in getting the word, or so he had read somewhere) was cocked at a terrible crooked angle, like the head of a hanged man. "He'd been with the Inn for thirty-five years, as I'm sure he told every guest he ever checked in. Most of them twice."

That tight little accent grated on Clay's frayed nerves. He thought that if it had been a fart, it would have been the kind that comes out sounding like a party-horn blown by a kid with asthma.

"A man came out of the elevator," the desk clerk said, once more using the pass-through to get behind the desk. Back there was apparently where he felt at home. The overhead light struck his face and Clay saw he was very pale. "One of the crazy ones. Franklin had the bad luck to be standing right there in front of the doors—"

"I don't suppose it crossed your mind to at least take the damn picture off his ass," Clay said. He bent down, picked up the Currier & Ives print, and put it on the couch. At the same time, he brushed the dead bellman's foot off the cushion where it had come to rest. It fell with a sound Clay knew very well. He had rendered it in a great many comic books as CLUMP.

"The man from the elevator only hit him with one punch," the desk clerk said. "It knocked poor Franklin all the way against the wall. I think it broke his neck. In any case, that was what dislodged the picture, Franklin striking the wall."

In the desk clerk's mind, this seemed to justify everything.

"What about the man who hit him?" Tom asked. "The crazy guy? Where'd he go?"

"Out," the desk clerk said. "That was when I felt locking the door to be by far the wisest course. After he went out." He looked at them with a combination of fear and prurient, gossipy greed that Clay found singularly distasteful. "What's *happening* out there? How bad has it gotten?"

"I think you must have a pretty good idea," Clay said. "Isn't that why you locked the door?"

"Yes, but—"

"What are they saying on TV?" Tom asked.

"Nothing. The cable's been out—" He glanced at his watch. "For almost half an hour now."

"What about the radio?"

The desk clerk gave Tom a prissy *you-must-be-joking* look. Clay was starting to think this guy could write a book—*How to Be Disliked on Short Notice.* "Radio in *this* place? In *any* downtown hotel? You must be joking."

From outside came a high-pitched wail of fear. The girl in the bloodstained white dress appeared at the door again and began pounding on it with the flat of her hand, looking over her shoulder as she did so. Clay started for her, fast.

"No, he locked it again, remember?" Tom shouted at him.

Clay hadn't. He turned to the desk clerk. "Unlock it."

"No," the desk clerk said, and crossed both arms firmly over his narrow chest to show how firmly he meant to oppose this course of action. Outside, the girl in the white dress looked over her shoulder again and pounded harder. Her blood-streaked face was tight with terror.

Clay pulled the butcher knife out of his belt. He had almost forgotten it and was sort of astonished at how quickly, how naturally, it returned to mind. "Open it, you sonofabitch," he told the desk clerk, "or I'll cut your throat."

10

"No time!" Tom yelled, and grabbed one of the high-backed, bogus Queen Anne chairs that flanked the lobby sofa. He ran it at the double doors with the legs up.

The girl saw him coming and cringed away, raising both of her hands to protect her face. At the same instant the man who had been chasing her appeared in front of the door. He was an enormous construction-worker type with a slab of a gut pushing out the front of his yellow T-shirt and a greasy salt-and-pepper pony-tail bouncing up and down on the back of it.

The chair-legs hit the panes of glass in the double doors, the two legs on the left shattering through **ATLANTIC AVENUE INN** and the two on the right through **BOSTON'S FINEST ADDRESS**. The ones on the right punched into the construction-worker type's meaty, yellow-clad left shoulder just as he grabbed the girl by the neck. The underside of the chair's seat fetched up against the solid seam where the two doors met and Tom McCourt went staggering backward, dazed.

The construction-worker guy was roaring out that speaking-in-tongues gibberish, and blood had begun to course down the freckled meat of his left biceps. The girl managed to pull free of him, but her feet tangled together and she went down in a heap, half on the sidewalk and half in the gutter, crying out in pain and fear.

Clay was standing framed in one of the shattered glass door-panels with no memory of crossing the room and only the vaguest one of raking the chair out of his way. "Hey dickweed!" he shouted, and was marginally encouraged when the big man's flood of crazy-talk ceased for a moment and he froze in his tracks. "Yeah, you!" Clay shouted. "I'm talking to you!" And then, because it was the only thing he could think of: "I fucked your mama, and she was one dry hump!"

The large maniac in the yellow shirt cried out something that sounded eerily like what the Power Suit Woman had cried out just before meeting her end— eerily like *Rast!*—and whirled back toward the building that had suddenly grown teeth and a voice and attacked him. Whatever he saw, it couldn't have been a grim, sweaty-faced man with a knife in his hand leaning out through a rectangular panel that had lately held glass, because Clay had to do no attacking at all. The man in the yellow shirt leaped *onto* the jutting blade of the butcher knife. The Swedish steel slid smoothly into the hanging, sunburned wattle beneath his chin and released a red waterfall. It doused Clay's hand, amazingly hot—almost hot as a freshly poured cup of coffee, it seemed—and he had to fight off an urge to pull away. Instead he pushed forward, at last feeling the knife encounter resistance. It hesitated, but there was no buckle in that baby. It ripped through gristle, then came out through the nape of the big man's neck. He fell forward—Clay couldn't hold him back with one arm, no way in hell, the guy had to go two-sixty, maybe even two-ninety—and for a moment leaned against the door like a drunk against a lamppost, brown eyes bulging, nicotine-stained tongue hanging from one corner of his mouth, neck spewing. Then his knees came unhinged and he went down. Clay held on to the handle of the knife and was amazed at how easily it came back out. Much easier than pulling it back through the leather and reinforced particleboard of the portfolio.

With the lunatic down he could see the girl again, one knee on the sidewalk and the other in the gutter, screaming through the curtain of hair hanging across her face.

"Honey," he said. "Honey, don't." But she went on screaming.

11

Her name was Alice Maxwell. She could tell them that much. And she could tell them that she and her mother had come into Boston on the train—from Boxford, she said—to do some shopping, a thing they often did on Wednesday, which she called her "short day" at the high school she attended. She said they'd gotten off the train at South Station and grabbed a cab. She said the cabdriver had been wearing a blue turban. She said the blue turban was the last thing she could remember until the bald desk clerk had finally unlocked the shattered double doors of the Atlantic Avenue Inn and let her in.

Clay thought she remembered more. He based this on the way she began to tremble when Tom McCourt asked her if either she or her mother had been carrying a cell phone. She claimed not to remember, but Clay was sure one or both of them had been. Everyone did these days, it seemed. He was just the exception that proved the rule. And there was Tom, who might owe his life to the cat that had knocked his off the counter.

They conversed with Alice (the conversation consisted for the most part of Clay asking questions while the girl sat mutely, looking down at her scraped knees and shaking her head from time to time) in the hotel lobby. Clay and Tom had moved Franklin's body behind the reception desk, dismissing the bald clerk's loud and bizarre protest that "it will just be under my feet there." The clerk, who had given his name simply as Mr. Ricardi, had since retired to his inner office. Clay had followed him just long enough to ascertain that Mr. Ricardi had been telling the truth about the TV being out of commish, then left him there. Sharon Riddell would have said Mr. Ricardi was brooding in his tent.

The man hadn't let Clay go without a parting shot, however. "Now we're open to the world," he said bitterly. "I hope you think you've accomplished something."

"Mr. Ricardi," Clay said, as patiently as he could, "I saw a plane crash-land on the other side of Boston Common not an hour ago. It sounds like more planes—big ones—are doing the same thing at Logan. Maybe they're even making suicide runs on the terminals. There are explosions all over downtown. I'd say that this afternoon all of Boston is open to the world."

As if to underline this point, a very heavy thump had come from above them. Mr. Ricardi didn't look up. He only flapped a *begone* hand in Clay's direction. With no TV to look at, he sat in his desk chair and looked severely at the wall.

12

Clay and Tom moved the two bogus Queen Anne chairs against the door, where their high backs did a pretty good job of filling the shattered frames that had once held glass. While Clay was sure that locking the hotel off from the street offered flimsy or outright false security, he thought that blocking the *view* from the street might be a good idea, and Tom had concurred. Once the chairs were in place, they lowered the sun-blind over the lobby's main window. That dimmed the room considerably and sent faint prison-bar shadows marching across the turkey-red rug.

With these things seen to, and Alice Maxwell's radically abridged tale told, Clay finally went to the telephone behind the desk. He glanced at his watch. It was 4:22 p.m., a perfectly logical time for it to be, except any ordinary sense of time seemed to have been canceled. It felt like hours since he'd seen the man biting the dog in the park. It also seemed like no time at all. But there *was* time, such as humans measured it, anyway, and in Kent Pond, Sharon would surely be back by now at the house he still thought of as home. He needed to talk to her. To make sure she was all right and tell her he was, too, but those weren't the important things. Making sure Johnny was all right, that was important, but there was something even more important than that. Vital, really.

He didn't have a cell phone, and neither did Sharon, he was almost positive of that. She might have picked one up since they'd separated in April, he supposed, but they still lived in the same town, he saw her almost every day, and he thought if she'd picked one up, he would have known. For one thing, she would have given him the number, right? Right. But—

But Johnny had one. Little Johnny-Gee, who wasn't so little anymore, twelve wasn't so little, and that was what he'd wanted for his last birthday. A red cell phone that played the theme music from his favorite TV program when it rang. Of course he was forbidden to turn it on or even take it out of his backpack when he was in school, but school hours were over now. Also, Clay and Sharon actually *encouraged* him to take it, partly because of the separation. There might be emergencies, or minor inconveniences such as a missed bus. What Clay had to hang on to was how Sharon had said she'd look into Johnny's room lately and more often than not see the cell lying forgotten on his desk or the windowsill beside his bed, off the charger and dead as dogshit.

Still, the thought of John's red cell phone ticked away in his mind like a bomb.

Clay touched the landline phone on the hotel desk, then withdrew his hand. Outside, something else exploded, but this one was distant. It was like hearing an artillery shell explode when you were well behind the lines.

Don't make that assumption, he thought. *Don't even assume there are lines.*

He looked across the lobby and saw Tom squatting beside Alice as she sat on the sofa. He was murmuring to her quietly, touching one of her loafers and looking up into her face. That was good. *He* was good. Clay was increasingly glad he'd run into Tom McCourt . . . or that Tom McCourt had run into him.

The landlines were probably all right. The question was whether probably was good enough. He had a wife who was still sort of his responsibility, and when it came to his son there was no sort-of at all. Even thinking of Johnny was dangerous. Every time his mind turned to the boy, Clay felt a panic-rat inside his mind, ready to burst free of the flimsy cage that held it and start gnawing anything it could get at with its sharp little teeth. If he could make sure Johnny and Sharon were okay, he could keep the rat in its cage and plan what to do next. But if he did something stupid, he wouldn't be able to help anyone. In fact, he would make things worse for the people here. He thought about this a little and then called the desk clerk's name.

When there was no answer from the inner office, he

called again. When there was still no answer, he said, "I know you hear me, Mr. Ricardi. If you make me come in there and get you, it'll annoy me. I might get annoyed enough to consider putting you out on the street."

"You can't do that," Mr. Ricardi said in a tone of surly instruction. "You are a *guest* of the *hotel*."

Clay thought of repeating what Tom had said to him while they were still outside—*things have changed.* Something made him keep silent instead.

"What," Mr. Ricardi said at last. Sounding more surly than ever. From overhead came a louder thump, as if someone had dropped a heavy piece of furniture. A bureau, maybe. This time even the girl looked up. Clay thought he heard a muffled shout—or maybe a howl of pain—but if so, there was no follow-up. What was on the second floor? Not a restaurant, he remembered being told (by Mr. Ricardi himself, when Clay checked in) that the hotel didn't have a restaurant, but the Metropolitan Café was right next door. *Meeting rooms,* he thought. *I'm pretty sure it's meeting rooms with Indian names.*

"*What?*" Mr. Ricardi asked again. He sounded grouchier than ever.

"Did you try to call anyone when all this started happening?"

"Well of *course*!" Mr. Ricardi said. He came to the door between the inner office and the area behind the reception desk, with its pigeonholes, security monitors, and its bank of computers. There he looked at Clay indignantly. "The fire alarms went off—I got *them* stopped, Doris said it was a wastebasket fire on the third floor—and I called the Fire Department to tell them not to bother. The line was busy! *Busy,* can you imagine!"

"You must have been very upset," Tom said.

Mr. Ricardi looked mollified for the first time. "I called the police when things outside started . . . you know . . . to go downhill."

"Yes," Clay said. *To go downhill* was one way of putting it, all right. "Did you get an answer?"

"A man told me I'd have to clear the line and then hung up on me," Mr. Ricardi said. The indignation was creeping back into his voice. "When I called again— this was after the crazy man came out of the elevator and killed Franklin—a woman answered. She said . . ." Mr. Ricardi's voice had begun to quiver and Clay saw the first tears running down the narrow defiles that marked the sides of the man's nose. ". . . said . . ."

"What?" Tom asked, in that same tone of mild sympathy. "What did she say, Mr. Ricardi?"

"She said if Franklin was dead and the man who killed him had run away, then I didn't have a problem. It was she who advised me to lock myself in. She also told me to call the hotel's elevators to lobby level and shut them off, which I did."

Clay and Tom exchanged a look that carried a wordless thought: *Good idea.* Clay got a sudden vivid image of bugs trapped between a closed window and a screen, buzzing furiously but unable to get out. This picture had something to do with the thumps they'd heard coming from above them. He wondered briefly how long before the thumper or thumpers up there would find the stairs.

"Then *she* hung up on me. After that, I called my wife in Milton."

"You got through to her," Clay said, wanting to be clear on this.

"She was very frightened. She asked me to come

home. I told her I had been advised to stay inside with the doors locked. Advised by the police. I told her to do the same thing. Lock up and keep a, you know, low profile. She *begged* me to come home. She said there had been gunshots on the street, and an explosion a street over. She said she had seen a naked man running through the Benzycks' yard. The Benzycks live next door to us."

"Yes," Tom said mildly. Soothingly, even. Clay said nothing. He was a bit ashamed at how angry he'd been at Mr. Ricardi, but Tom had been angry, too.

"She said she believed the naked man might—*might,* she only said *might*—have been carrying the body of a . . . mmm . . . nude child. But possibly it was a doll. She begged me again to leave the hotel and come home."

Clay had what he needed. The landlines were safe. Mr. Ricardi was in shock but not crazy. Clay put his hand on the telephone. Mr. Ricardi laid his hand over Clay's before Clay could pick up the receiver. Mr. Ricardi's fingers were long and pale and very cold. Mr. Ricardi wasn't done. Mr. Ricardi was on a roll.

"She called me a son of a bitch and hung up. I know she was angry with me, and of course I understand why. But the police told me to lock up and stay put. The police told me to keep off the streets. The police. The *authorities.*"

Clay nodded. "The authorities, sure."

"Did you come by the T?" Mr. Ricardi asked. "I always use the T. It's just two blocks down the street. It's very convenient."

"It wouldn't be convenient this afternoon," Tom said. "After what we just saw, you couldn't get me down there on a bet."

Mr. Ricardi looked at Clay with mournful eagerness. "You see?"

Clay nodded again. "You're better off in here," he said. Knowing that he meant to get home and see to his boy. Sharon too, of course, but mostly his boy. Knowing he would let nothing stop him unless something absolutely did. It was like a weight in his mind that cast an actual shadow on his vision. "Much better off." Then he picked up the phone and punched 9 for an outside line. He wasn't sure he'd get one, but he did. He dialed 1, then 207, the area code for all of Maine, and then 692, which was the prefix for Kent Pond and the surrounding towns. He got three of the last four numbers—almost to the house he still thought of as home—before the distinctive three-tone interrupt. A recorded female voice followed. "We're sorry. All circuits are busy. Please try your call again later."

On the heels of this came a dial tone as some automated circuit disconnected him from Maine . . . if that was where the robot voice had been coming from. Clay let the handset drop to the level of his shoulder, as if it had grown very heavy. Then he put it back in the cradle.

13

Tom told him he was crazy to want to leave.

For one thing, he pointed out, they were relatively safe here in the Atlantic Avenue Inn, especially with the elevators locked down and lobby access from the stairwell blocked off. This they had done by piling boxes and suitcases from the luggage room in front of the door at the end of the short corridor beyond the elevator banks. Even if someone of extraordinary strength were to push against that door from the other side, he'd only be able to shift the pile against the facing wall, creating a gap of maybe six inches. Not enough to get through.

For another, the tumult in the city beyond their little safe haven actually seemed to be increasing. There was a constant racket of conflicting alarms, shouts and screams and racing engines, and sometimes the panic-tang of smoke, although the day's brisk breeze seemed to be carrying the worst of that away from them. *So far,* Clay thought, but did not say aloud, at least not yet— he didn't want to frighten the girl any more than she already was. There were explosions that never seemed to come singly but rather in spasms. One of those was so close that they all ducked, sure the front window would blow in. It didn't, but after that they moved to Mr. Ricardi's inner sanctum.

The third reason Tom gave for thinking Clay was crazy to even *think* about leaving the marginal safety of the Inn was that it was now quarter past five. The day would be ending soon. He argued that trying to leave Boston in the dark would be madness.

"Just take a gander out there," he said, gesturing to Mr. Ricardi's little window, which looked out on Essex Street. Essex was crowded with abandoned cars. There was also at least one body, that of a young woman in jeans and a Red Sox sweatshirt. She lay facedown on the sidewalk, both arms outstretched, as if she had died try-ing to swim. VARITEK, her sweatshirt proclaimed. "Do you think you're going to drive your car? If you do, you better think again."

"He's right," Mr. Ricardi said. He was sitting behind his desk with his arms once more folded across his nar-row chest, a study in gloom. "You're in the Tamworth Street Parking Garage. I doubt if you'd even succeed in securing your keys."

CELL 55

Clay, who had already given his car up as a lost cause, opened his mouth to say he wasn't planning to drive (at least to start with), when another thump came from overhead, this one heavy enough to make the ceiling shiver. It was accompanied by the faint but distinctive shiver-jingle of breaking glass. Alice Maxwell, who was sitting in the chair across the desk from Mr. Ricardi, looked up nervously and then seemed to shrink further into herself.

"What's up there?" Tom asked.

"It's the Iroquois Room directly overhead," Mr. Ricardi replied. "The largest of our three meeting rooms, and where we keep all of our supplies—chairs, tables, audio-visual equipment." He paused. "And, although we have no restaurant, we arrange for buffets or cocktail parties, if clients request such service. That last thump . . ."

He didn't finish. As far as Clay was concerned, he didn't need to. That last thump had been a trolley stacked high with glassware being upended on the floor of the Iroquois Room, where numerous other trolleys and tables had already been tipped over by some madman who was rampaging back and forth up there. Buzzing around on the second floor like a bug trapped between the window and the screen, something without the wit to find a way out, something that could only run and break, run and break.

Alice spoke up for the first time in nearly half an hour, and without prompting for the first time since they'd met her. "You said something about someone named Doris."

"Doris Gutierrez." Mr. Ricardi was nodding. "The head housekeeper. Excellent employee. Probably my best. She was on three, the last time I heard from her."

"Did she have—?" Alice wouldn't say it. Instead she

made a gesture that had become almost as familiar to Clay as the index finger across the lips indicating *Shh*. Alice put her right hand to the side of her face with the thumb close to her ear and the pinkie in front of her mouth.

"No," Mr. Ricardi said, almost primly. "Employees have to leave them in their lockers while they're on the job. One violation gets them a reprimand. Two and they can be fired. I tell them this when they're taken on." He lifted one thin shoulder in a half-shrug. "It's management's policy, not mine."

"Would she have gone down to the second floor to investigate those sounds?" Alice asked.

"Possibly," Mr. Ricardi said. "I have no way of knowing. I only know that I haven't heard from her since she reported the wastebasket fire out, and she hasn't answered her pages. I paged her twice."

Clay didn't want to say *You see, it isn't safe here, either* right out loud, so he looked past Alice at Tom, trying to give him the basic idea with his eyes.

Tom said, "How many people would you say are still upstairs?"

"I have no way of knowing."

"If you had to guess."

"Not many. As far as the housekeeping staff goes, probably just Doris. The day crew leaves at three, and the night crew doesn't come on until six." Mr. Ricardi pressed his lips tightly together. "It's an economy gesture. One cannot say *measure* because it doesn't work. As for guests . . ."

He considered.

"Afternoon is a slack time for us, very slack. Last night's guests have all checked out, of course—checkout time at the Atlantic Inn is noon—and tonight's guests wouldn't begin checking in until four o'clock or so, on an ordinary afternoon. Which this most definitely is not. Guests staying several days are usually here on business. As I assume *you* were, Mr. Riddle."

Clay nodded without bothering to correct Ricardi on his name.

"At midafternoon, businesspeople are usually out doing whatever it was that brought them to Boston. So you see, we have the place almost to ourselves."

As if to contradict this, there came another thump from above them, more shattering glass, and a faint feral growl. They all looked up.

"Clay, listen," Tom said. "If the guy up there finds the stairs . . . I don't know if these people are capable of thought, but—"

"Judging by what we saw on the street," Clay said, "even calling them people might be wrong. I've got an idea that guy up there is more like a bug trapped between a window and a screen. A bug trapped like that might get out—if it found a hole—and the guy up there might find the stairs, but if he does, I think it'll be by accident."

"And when he gets down and finds the door to the lobby blocked, he'll use the fire-door to the alley," Mr. Ricardi said with what was, for him, eagerness. "We'll hear the alarm—it's rigged to ring when anyone pushes the bar—and we'll know he's gone. One less nut to worry about."

Somewhere south of them something big blew up, and they all cringed. Clay supposed he now knew what living in Beirut during the 1980s had been like.

"I'm trying to make a point here," he said patiently.

"I don't think so," Tom said. "You're going anyway, because you're worried about your wife and son. You're trying to persuade us because you want company."

Clay blew out a frustrated breath. "Sure I want company, but that's not why I'm trying to talk you into coming. The smell of smoke's stronger, but when's the last time you heard a siren?"

None of them replied.

"Me either," Clay said. "I don't think things are going to get better in Boston, not for a while. They're going to get worse. If it *was* the cell phones—"

"She tried to leave a message for Dad," Alice said. She spoke rapidly, as if wanting to make sure she got all the words out before the memory flew away. "She just wanted to make sure he'd pick up the dry cleaning because she needed her yellow wool dress for her committee meeting and I needed my extra uni for the away game on Saturday. This was in the cab. And then we crashed! *She choked the man and she bit the man and his turban fell off and there was blood on the side of his face and we crashed!*"

Alice looked around at their three staring faces, then put her own face in her hands and began to sob. Tom moved to comfort her, but Mr. Ricardi surprised Clay by coming around his desk and putting one pipestemmy arm around the girl before Tom could get to her. "There-there," he said. "I'm sure it was all a misunderstanding, young lady."

She looked up at him, her eyes wide and wild. *"Misunderstanding?"* She indicated the dried bib of blood on the front of her dress. "Does this look like a *misunderstanding*? I used the karate from the self-defense classes I took in junior high. I used karate on my own mother! I broke her nose, I think . . . I'm *sure* . . ." Alice shook her head rapidly, her hair flying. "And still, if I hadn't been able to reach behind me and get the door open . . ."

"She would have killed you," Clay said flatly.

"She would have killed me," Alice agreed in a whisper. "She didn't know who I was. My own mother." She looked from Clay to Tom. "It was the cell phones," she said in that same whisper. "It was the cell phones, all right."

14

"So how many of the damn things are there in Boston?" Clay asked. "What's the market penetration?"

"Given the large numbers of college students, I'd say it's got to be huge," Mr. Ricardi replied. He had resumed his seat behind his desk, and now he looked a little more animated. Comforting the girl might have done it, or perhaps it was being asked a business-oriented question. "Although it goes much further than affluent young people, of course. I read an article in *Inc.* only a month or two ago that claimed there's now as many cell phones in mainland China as there are people in America. Can you imagine?"

Clay didn't want to imagine.

"All right." Tom was nodding reluctantly. "I see where you're going with this. Someone—some terrorist outfit—rigs the cell phone signals somehow. If you make a call or take one, you get some kind of a . . . what? . . . some kind of a subliminal message, I guess . . . that makes you crazy. Sounds like science fiction, but I suppose fifteen or twenty years ago, cell phones as they now exist would have seemed like science fiction to most people."

"I'm pretty sure it's something like that," Clay said. "You can get enough of it to screw you up righteously if you even *overhear* a call." He was thinking of Pixie Dark. "But the insidious thing is that when people see things going wrong all around them—"

"Their first impulse is to reach for their cell phones and try to find out what's causing it," Tom said.

"Yeah," Clay said. "I saw people doing it."

Tom looked at him bleakly. "So did I."

"What all this has to do with you leaving the safety of the hotel, especially with dark coming on, I don't know," Mr. Ricardi said.

As if in answer, there came another explosion. It was followed by half a dozen more, marching off to the southeast like the diminishing footsteps of a giant. From above them came another thud, and a faint cry of rage.

"I don't think the crazy ones will have the brains to leave the city any more than that guy up there can find his way to the stairs," Clay said.

For a moment he thought the look on Tom's face was shock, and then he realized it was something else. Amazement, maybe. And dawning hope. "Oh, Christ," he said, and actually slapped the side of his face with one hand. "*They* won't leave. I never thought of that."

"There might be something else," Alice said. She was biting her lip and looking down at her hands, which were working together in a restless knot. She forced herself to look up at Clay. "It might actually be *safer* to go after dark."

"Why's that, Alice?"

"If they can't see you—if you can get behind something, if you can hide—they forget about you almost right away."

"What makes you think that, honey?" Tom asked.

"Because I hid from the man who was chasing me," she said in a low voice. "The guy in the yellow shirt. This was just before I saw you. I hid in an alley. Behind one of those Dumpster thingies? I was scared, because I thought there might not be any way back out if he came in after me, but it was all I could think of to do. I saw him standing at the mouth of the alley, looking around, *walking* around and around—walking the worry-circle, my grampa would say—and at first I thought he was playing with me, you know? Because he *had* to've seen me go into the alley, I was only a few feet ahead of him . . . just a few feet . . . almost close enough to grab . . ." Alice began to tremble. "But once I was in there, it was like . . . I dunno . . ."

"Out of sight, out of mind," Tom said. "But if he was that close, why did you stop running?"

"Because I couldn't anymore," Alice said. "I just couldn't. My legs were like rubber, and I felt like I was going to shake myself apart from the inside. But it turned out I didn't have to run, anyway. He walked the worry-circle a few more times, muttering that crazy talk, and then just walked off. I could hardly believe it. I thought he had to be trying to fake me out . . . but at the same time I knew he was too crazy for anything like that." She glanced briefly at Clay, then back down at her hands again. "My problem was running into him again. I should have stuck with you guys the first time. I can be pretty stupid sometimes."

"You were sca—" Clay began, and then the biggest explosion yet came from somewhere east of them, a deafening *KER-WHAM!* that made them all duck and cover their ears. They heard the window in the lobby shatter.

"My . . . *God,*" Mr. Ricardi said. His wide eyes underneath that bald head made him look to Clay like Little Orphan Annie's mentor, Daddy Warbucks. "That might have been the new Shell superstation they put in over on Kneeland. The one all the taxis and the Duck Boats use. It was the right direction."

Clay had no idea if Ricardi was right, he couldn't smell burning gasoline (at least not yet), but his visually trained mind's eye could see a triangle of city concrete now burning like a propane torch in the latening day.

"Can a modern city burn?" he asked Tom. "One made mostly of concrete and metal and glass? Could it burn the way Chicago did after Mrs. O'Leary's cow kicked over the lantern?"

"That lantern-kicking business was nothing but an urban legend," Alice said. She was rubbing the back of her neck as if she were getting a bad headache. "Mrs. Myers said so, in American History."

"Sure it could," Tom said. "Look what happened to the World Trade Center, after those airplanes hit it."

"Airplanes full of jet fuel," Mr. Ricardi said pointedly.

As if the bald desk clerk had conjured it, the smell of burning gasoline began to come to them, wafting through the shattered lobby windows and sliding beneath the door to the inner office like bad mojo.

"I guess you were on the nose about that Shell station," Tom remarked.

Mr. Ricardi went to the door between his office and the lobby. He unlocked it and opened it. What Clay could see of the lobby beyond already looked deserted and gloomy and somehow irrelevant. Mr. Ricardi sniffed audibly, then closed the door and locked it again. "Fainter already," he said.

"Wishful thinking," Clay said. "Either that or your nose is getting used to the aroma."

"I think he might be right," Tom said. "That's a good west wind out there—by which I mean the air's moving toward the ocean—and if what we just heard was that new station they put in on the corner of Kneeland and Washington, by the New England Medical Center—"

"That's the one, all right," Mr. Ricardi said. His face registered glum satisfaction. "Oh, the protests! The smart money fixed *that,* believe you m—"

Tom overrode him. "—then the hospital will be on fire by now . . . along with anybody left inside, of course . . ."

"No," Alice said, then put a hand over her mouth.

"I think yes. And the Wang Center's next in line. The breeze may drop by full dark, but if it doesn't, everything east of the Mass Pike is apt to be so much toasted cheese by ten p.m."

"We're *west* of there," Mr. Ricardi pointed out.

"Then we're safe enough," Clay said. "At least from *that* one." He went to Mr. Ricardi's little window, stood on his toes, and peered out onto Essex Street.

"What do you see?" Alice asked. "Do you see people?"

"No . . . yes. One man. Other side of the street."

"Is he one of the crazy ones?" she asked.

"I can't tell." But Clay thought he was. It was the way he ran, and the jerky way he kept looking back over his shoulder. Once, just before he went around the corner and onto Lincoln Street, the guy almost ran into a fruit display in front of a grocery store. And although Clay couldn't hear him, he could see the man's lips moving. "Now he's gone."

"No one else?" Tom asked.

"Not at the moment, but there's smoke." Clay paused. "Soot and ash, too. I can't tell how much. The wind's whipping it around."

"Okay, I'm convinced," Tom said. "I've always been a slow learner but never a no-learner. The city's going to burn and nobody's going to stand pat but the crazy people."

"I think that's right," Clay said. And he didn't think

this was true of just Boston, but for the time being, Boston was all he could bear to consider. In time he might be able to widen his view, but not until he knew Johnny was safe. Or maybe the big picture was always going to be beyond him. He drew small pictures for a living, after all. But in spite of everything, the selfish fellow who lived like a limpet on the underside of his mind had time to send up a clear thought. It came in colors of blue and dark sparkling gold. *Why did it have to happen today, of all days? Just after I finally made a solid strike?*

"Can I come with you guys, if you go?" Alice asked.

"Sure," Clay said. He looked at the desk clerk. "You can, too, Mr. Ricardi."

"I shall stay at my post," Mr. Ricardi said. He spoke loftily, but before they shifted away from Clay's, his eyes looked sick.

"I don't think you'll get in Dutch with the management for locking up and leaving under these circumstances," Tom said. He spoke in the gentle fashion Clay was so much coming to like.

"I shall stay at my post," he said again. "Mr. Donnelly, the day manager, went out to make the afternoon deposit at the bank and left me in charge. If he comes back, perhaps then . . ."

"Please, Mr. Ricardi," Alice said. "Staying here is no good."

But Mr. Ricardi, who had once more crossed his arms over his thin chest, only shook his head.

15

They moved one of the Queen Anne chairs aside, and Mr. Ricardi unlocked the front doors for them. Clay looked out. He could see no people moving in either direction, but it was hard to tell for sure because the air was now full of fine dark ash. It danced in the breeze like black snow.

"Come on," he said. They were only going next door to start with, to the Metropolitan Café.

"I'm going to relock the door and put the chair back in place," Mr. Ricardi said, "but I'll be listening. If you run into trouble—if there are more of those . . . *people* . . . hiding in the Metropolitan, for instance—and you have to retreat, just remember to shout, 'Mr. Ricardi, Mr. Ricardi, we need you!' That way I'll know it's safe to open the door. Is that understood?"

"Yes," Clay said. He squeezed Mr. Ricardi's thin shoulder. The desk clerk flinched, then stood firm (although he showed no particular sign of pleasure at being so saluted). "You're all right. I didn't think you were, but I was wrong."

"I hope I do my best," the bald man said stiffly. "Just remember—"

"We'll remember," Tom said. "And we'll be over there maybe ten minutes. If anything goes wrong over here, *you* give a shout."

"All right." But Clay didn't think he would. He didn't know why he thought that, it made no sense to think a man wouldn't give a shout to save himself if he was in trouble, but Clay *did* think it.

Alice said, "*Please* change your mind, Mr. Ricardi. It's not safe in Boston, you must know that by now."

Mr. Ricardi only looked away. And Clay thought, not without wonder, *This is how a man looks when he's deciding that the risk of death is better than the risk of change.*

"Come on," Clay said. "Let's make some sandwiches while we've still got electricity to see by."

"Some bottled water wouldn't hurt, either," Tom said.

16

The electricity failed just as they were wrapping the last of their sandwiches in the Metropolitan Café's tidy, white-tiled little kitchen. By then Clay had tried three more times to get through to Maine: once to his old house, once to Kent Pond Elementary, where Sharon taught, and once to Joshua Chamberlain Middle School, which Johnny now attended. In no case did he get further than Maine's 207 area code.

When the lights in the Metropolitan went out, Alice screamed in what at first seemed to Clay like total darkness. Then the emergency lights came on. Alice was not much comforted. She was clinging to Tom with one arm. In the other she was brandishing the bread-knife she'd used to cut the sandwiches with. Her eyes were wide and somehow flat.

"Alice, put that knife down," Clay said, a little more harshly than he'd intended. "Before you cut one of us with it."

"Or yourself," Tom said in that mild and soothing voice of his. His spectacles glinted in the glare of the emergency lights.

She put it down, then promptly picked it up again. "I want it," she said. "I want to take it with me. You have one, Clay. I want one."

"All right," he said, "but you don't have a belt. We'll make you one from a tablecloth. For now, just be careful."

Half the sandwiches were roast beef and cheese, half ham and cheese. Alice had wrapped them in Saran Wrap. Under the cash register Clay found a stack of sacks with DOGGY BAG written on one side and PEOPLE BAG written on the other. He and Tom tumbled the sandwiches into a pair of these. Into a third bag they put three bottles of water.

The tables had been made up for a dinner-service that was never going to happen. Two or three had been tumbled over but most stood perfect, with their glasses and silver shining in the hard light of the emergency boxes on the walls. Something about their calm orderliness hurt Clay's heart. The cleanliness of the folded napkins, and the little electric lamps on each table. Those were now dark, and he had an idea it might be a long time before the bulbs inside lit up again.

He saw Alice and Tom gazing about with faces as unhappy as his felt, and a desire to cheer them up—almost manic in its urgency—came over him. He remembered a trick he used to do for his son. He wondered again about Johnny's cell phone and the panic-rat took another nip out of him. Clay hoped with all his heart the damned phone was lying forgotten under Johnny-Gee's bed among the dust-kitties, with its battery flat-flat-flat.

"Watch this carefully," he said, setting his bag of sandwiches aside, "and please note that at no time do my hands leave my wrists." He grasped the hanging skirt of a tablecloth.

"This is hardly the time for parlor tricks," Tom said.

"I want to see," Alice said. For the first time since they'd met her, there was a smile on her face. It was small but it was there.

"We need the tablecloth," Clay said, "it won't take a second, and besides, the lady wants to see." He turned to Alice. "But you have to say a magic word. *Shazam* will do."

"Shazam!" she said, and Clay pulled briskly with both hands.

He hadn't done the trick in two, maybe even three years, and it almost didn't work. And yet at the same time, his mistake—some small hesitation in the pull, no doubt—actually added to the charm of the thing. Instead of staying where they were while the tablecloth magically disappeared from beneath them, all the place-settings on the table moved about four inches to the right. The glass nearest to where Clay was standing actually wound up with its circular base half on and half off the table.

Alice applauded, now laughing. Clay took a bow with his hands held out.

"Can we go now, O great Vermicelli?" Tom asked, but even Tom was smiling. Clay could see his small teeth in the emergency lights.

"Soon's I rig this," Clay said. "She can carry the knife on one side and a bag of sandwiches on the other. You can tote the water." He folded the tablecloth over into a triangle shape, then rolled it quickly into a belt. He slipped a bag of sandwiches onto this by the bag's carrier handles, then put the tablecloth around the girl's slim waist, having to take a turn and a half and tie the knot in back to make the thing secure. He finished by sliding the serrated bread-knife home on the right side.

"Say, you're pretty handy," Tom said.

"Handy is dandy," Clay said, and then something else blew up outside, close enough to shake the café. The glass that had been standing half on and half off the table lost its balance, tumbled to the floor, and shattered. The three of them looked at it. Clay thought to tell them he didn't believe in omens, but that would only make things worse. Besides, he did.

17

Clay had his reasons for wanting to go back to the Atlantic Avenue Inn before they set off. One was to retrieve his portfolio, which he'd left sitting in the lobby. Another was to see if they couldn't find some sort of makeshift scabbard for Alice's knife—he reckoned even a shaving kit would do, if it was long enough. A third was to give Mr. Ricardi another chance to join them. He was surprised to find he wanted this even more than he wanted the forgotten portfolio of drawings. He had taken an odd, reluctant liking to the man.

When he confessed this to Tom, Tom surprised him by nodding. "It's the way I feel about anchovies on pizza," he said. "I tell myself there's something disgusting about a combination of cheese, tomato sauce, and dead fish . . . but sometimes that shameful urge comes over me and I can't stand against it."

A blizzard of black ash and soot was blowing up the street and between the buildings. Car alarms warbled, burglar alarms brayed, and fire alarms clanged. There seemed to be no heat in the air, but Clay could hear the crackle of fire to the south and east of them. The smell of burning was stronger, too. They heard voices shouting, but these were back toward the Common, where Boylston Street widened.

When they got next door to the Atlantic Avenue Inn, Tom helped Clay push one of the Queen Anne chairs away from one of the broken glass door-panels. The lobby beyond was now a pool of gloom in which Mr. Ricardi's desk and the sofa were only darker shadows; if Clay hadn't already been in there, he would have had no idea what those shadows represented. Above the elevators a single emergency light guttered, the boxed battery beneath it buzzing like a horsefly.

"Mr. Ricardi?" Tom called. "Mr. Ricardi, we came back to see if you changed your mind."

There was no reply. After a moment, Alice began carefully to knock out the glass teeth that still jutted from the windowframe.

"Mr. Ricardi!" Tom called again, and when there was still no answer, he turned to Clay. "You're going in there, are you?"

"Yes. To get my portfolio. It's got my drawings in it."

"You don't have copies?"

"Those are the originals," Clay said, as if this explained everything. To him it did. And besides, there was Mr. Ricardi. He'd said, *I'll be listening.*

"What if Thumper from upstairs got him?" Tom asked.

"If that had happened, I think we'd have heard him thumping around down here," Clay said. "For that matter, he would have come running at the sound of our voices, babbling like the guy who tried to carve us up back by the Common."

"You don't know that," Alice said. She was gnawing at her lower lip. "It's way too early for you to think you know all the rules."

Of course she was right, but they couldn't stand around out here discussing it, that was no good, either.

"I'll be careful," he said, and put a leg over the bottom of the window. It was narrow, but plenty wide enough for him to climb through. "I'll just poke my head into his office. If he's not there, I won't go hunting around for him like a chick in a horror movie. I'll just grab my portfolio and we'll boogie."

"Keep yelling," Alice said. "Just say 'Okay, I'm okay,' something like that. The whole time."

"All right, but if I stop yelling, just *go*. Don't come in after me."

"Don't worry," she said, unsmiling. "I saw all those movies, too. We've got Cinemax."

18

"I'm okay," Clay shouted, picking up his portfolio and then putting it down on the reception desk. *Good to go,* he thought. But not quite yet.

He looked over his shoulder as he went around the desk and saw the one unblocked window glimmering, seeming to float in the thickening gloom, with two silhouettes cut into the day's last light. "I'm okay, still okay, just going in to check his office now, still okay, still o—"

"Clay?" Tom's voice was alarmed, but for a moment Clay couldn't respond and set Tom's mind at rest. There was an overhead light fixture in the middle of the inner office's high ceiling. Mr. Ricardi was hanging from it by what looked like a drape-cord. There was a white bag pulled down over his head. Clay thought it was the kind of plastic bag the hotel gave you to put your dirty laundry and dry cleaning in. "Clay, are you all right?"

"Clay?" Alice sounded shrill, ready to be hysterical.

"Okay," he heard himself say. His mouth seemed to be operating itself, with no help from his brain. "Still right here." He was thinking of how Mr. Ricardi had looked when he said *I shall stay at my post*. The words had been lofty, but the eyes had been scared and somehow humble, the eyes of a small raccoon driven into a corner of the garage by a large and angry dog. "I'm coming out now."

He backed away, as if Mr. Ricardi might slip his homemade drape-cord noose and come after him the second he turned his back. He was suddenly more than afraid for Sharon and Johnny; he was homesick for them with a depth of feeling that made him think of his first day at school, his mother leaving him at the playground gate. The other parents had walked their kids inside. But his mother said, *You just go in there, Clayton, it's the first room, you'll be fine, boys should do this part alone.* Before he did what she told him he had watched her going away, back up Cedar Street. Her blue coat. Now, standing here in the dark, he was renewing acquaintance with the knowledge that the second part of homesick was *sick* for a reason.

Tom and Alice were fine, but he wanted the people he loved.

Once he was around the reception desk, he faced the street and crossed the lobby. He got close enough to the long broken window to see the frightened faces of his new friends, then remembered he had forgotten his fucking portfolio again and had to go back. Reaching for it, he felt certain that Mr. Ricardi's hand would steal out of the gathering darkness behind the desk and close over his. That didn't happen, but from overhead came another of those thumps. Something still up there, something still blundering around in the dark. Something that had been human until three o'clock this afternoon.

This time when he was halfway to the door, the lobby's single battery-powered emergency light stuttered briefly, then went out. *That's a Fire Code violation,* Clay thought. *I ought to report that.*

He handed out his portfolio. Tom took it.

"Where is he?" Alice asked. "Wasn't he there?"

"Dead," Clay said. It had crossed his mind to lie, but he didn't think he was capable. He was too shocked by what he had seen. How did a man hang himself? He didn't see how it was even possible. "Suicide."

Alice began to cry, and it occurred to Clay that she didn't know that if it had been up to Mr. Ricardi, she'd probably be dead herself now. The thing was, he felt a little like crying himself. Because Mr. Ricardi had come around. Maybe most people did, if they got a chance.

From west of them on the darkening street, back toward the Common, came a scream that seemed too great to have issued from human lungs. It sounded to Clay almost like the trumpeting of an elephant. There was no pain in it, and no joy. There was only madness. Alice cringed against him, and he put an arm around her. The feel of her body was like the feel of an electrical wire with a strong current passing through it.

"If we're going to get out of here, let's do it," Tom said. "If we don't run into too much trouble, we should be able to get as far north as Malden, and spend the night at my place."

"That's a hell of a good idea," Clay said.

Tom smiled cautiously. "You really think so?"

"I really do. Who knows, maybe Officer Ashland's already there."

"Who's Officer Ashland?" Alice asked.

"A policeman we met back by the Common," Tom said. "He . . . you know, helped us out." The three of them were now walking east toward Atlantic Avenue, through the falling ash and the sound of alarms. "We won't see him, though. Clay's just trying to be funny."

"Oh," she said. "I'm glad somebody's trying to be." Lying on the pavement by a litter barrel was a blue cell phone with a cracked casing. Alice kicked it into the gutter without breaking stride.

"Good one," Clay said.

Alice shrugged. "Five years of soccer," she said, and at that moment the streetlights came on, like a promise that all was not yet lost.

MALDEN

Thousands of people stood on the Mystic River Bridge and watched as everything between Comm Ave and Boston Harbor took fire and burned. The wind from the west remained brisk and warm even after the sun was down and the flames roared like a furnace, blotting out the stars. The rising moon was full and ultimately hideous. Sometimes the smoke masked it, but all too often that bulging dragon's eye swam free and peered down, casting a bleary orange light. Clay thought it a horror-comic moon, but didn't say so.

No one had much to say. The people on the bridge only looked at the city they had so lately left, watching as the flames reached the pricey harborfront condos and began engulfing them. From across the water came an interwoven tapestry of alarms—fire alarms and car alarms, mostly, with several whooping sirens added for spice. For a while an amplified voice had told citizens to GET OFF THE STREETS, and then another had begun advising them to LEAVE THE CITY ON FOOT BY MAJOR ARTERIES WEST AND NORTH. These two contradictory pieces of advice had competed with each other for several minutes, and then GET OFF THE STREETS had ceased. About five minutes later, LEAVE THE CITY ON FOOT had also quit. Now there was only the hungry roar of the wind-driven fire, the alarms, and a steady low crumping sound that Clay thought must be windows imploding in the enormous heat.

He wondered how many people had been trapped over there. Trapped between the fire and the water.

"Remember wondering if a modern city could burn?" Tom McCourt said. In the light of the fire, his small, intelligent face looked tired and sick. There was a smudge of ash on one of his cheeks. "Remember that?"

"Shut up, come on," Alice said. She was clearly distraught, but like Tom, she spoke in a low voice. *It's like we're in a library,* Clay thought. And then he thought, *No—a funeral home.* "Can't we please go? Because this is kicking my ass."

"Sure," Clay said. "You bet. How far to your place, Tom?"

"From here, less than two miles," he said. "But it's not all behind us, I'm sorry to say." They had turned north now, and he pointed ahead and to the right. The glow blooming there could almost have been orange-tinted arc-sodium streetlights on a cloudy night, except the night was clear and the streetlights were now out. In any case, streetlights did not give off rising columns of smoke.

Alice moaned, then covered her mouth as if she expected someone among the silent multitude watching Boston burn might reprimand her for making too much noise.

"Don't worry," Tom said with eerie calm. "We're going to Malden and that looks like Revere. The way the wind's blowing, Malden should still be all right."

Stop right there, Clay urged him silently, but Tom did not.

"For now," he added.

2

There were several dozen abandoned cars on the lower deck of the span, and a fire truck with EAST BOSTON lettered on its avocado-green side that had been sideswiped by a cement truck (both were abandoned), but mostly this level of the bridge belonged to the pedestrians. *Except now you probably have to call them refugees,* Clay thought, and then realized there was no *them* about it. Us. *Call us refugees.*

There was still very little talk. Most people just stood and watched the city burn in silence. Those who *were* moving went slowly, looking back frequently over their shoulders. Then, as they neared the far end of the bridge (he could see *Old Ironsides*—at least he thought it was *Old Ironsides*—riding at anchor in the Harbor, still safe from the flames), he noticed an odd thing. Many of them were also looking at Alice. At first he had the paranoid idea that people must think he and Tom had abducted the girl and were spiriting her away for God knew what immoral purposes. Then he had to remind himself that these wraiths on the Mystic Bridge were in shock, even more uprooted from their normal lives than the Hurricane Katrina refugees had been—those unfortunates had at least had some warning—and were unlikely to be capable of considering such fine ideas. Most were too deep in their own heads for moralizing. Then the moon rose a little higher and came out a little more strongly, and he got it: she was the only adolescent in sight. Even Clay himself was young compared to most of their fellow refugees. The majority of people gawking at the torch that had been Boston or plodding slowly toward Malden and Danvers were over forty, and many looked eligible for the Golden Ager discount at

Denny's. He saw a few people with little kids, and a couple of babies in strollers, but that was pretty much it for the younger set.

A little farther on, he noticed something else. There were cell phones lying discarded in the roadway. Every few feet they passed another one, and none were whole. They had either been run over or stomped down to nothing but wire and splinters of plastic, like dangerous snakes that had been destroyed before they could bite again.

3

"What's your name, dear?" asked a plump woman who came angling across to their side of the highway. This was about five minutes after they had left the bridge. Tom said another fifteen would bring them to the Salem Street exit, and from there it was only four blocks to his house. He said his cat would be awfully glad to see him, and that had brought a wan smile to Alice's face. Clay thought wan was better than nothing.

Now Alice looked with reflexive mistrust at the plump woman who had detached herself from the mostly silent groups and little lines of men and women— hardly more than shadows, really, some with suitcases, some carrying shopping bags or wearing backpacks— that had crossed the Mystic and were walking north on Route One, away from the great fire to the south and all too aware of the new one taking hold in Revere, off to the northeast.

The plump woman looked back at her with sweet interest. Her graying hair was done in neat beauty-shop curls. She wore cat's-eye glasses and what Clay's mother would have called a "car coat." She carried a shopping bag in one hand and a book in the other. There seemed to be no harm in her. She certainly wasn't one of the phone-crazies—they hadn't seen a single one of those since leaving the Atlantic Avenue Inn with their sacks of grub—but Clay felt himself go on point, just the same. To be approached as if they were at a get-acquainted tea instead of fleeing a burning city didn't seem normal. But under these circumstances, just what was? He was probably losing it, but if so, Tom was, too. He was also watching the plump, motherly woman with go-away eyes.

"Alice?" Alice said at last, just when Clay had decided the girl wasn't going to reply at all. She sounded like a kid trying to answer what she fears may be a trick question in a class that's really too tough for her. "My name is Alice Maxwell?"

"Alice," the plump woman said, and her lips curved in a maternal smile as sweet as her look of interest. There was no reason that smile should have set Clay on edge more than he already was, but it did. "That's a lovely name. It means 'blessed of God.' "

"Actually, ma'am, it means 'of the royalty' or 'regally born,' " Tom said. "Now could you excuse us? The girl has just lost her mother today, and—"

"We've *all* lost someone today, haven't we, Alice?" the plump woman said without looking at Tom. She kept pace with Alice, her beauty-shop curls bouncing with every step. Alice was eyeing her with a mixture of unease and fascination. Around them others paced and sometimes hurried and often plodded with their heads down, little more than wraiths in this unaccustomed darkness, and Clay still saw nobody young except for a few babies, a few toddlers, and Alice. No adolescents because most adolescents had cell phones, like Pixie

Light back at the Mister Softee truck. Or like his own son, who had a red Nextel with a ring-tone from *The Monster Club* and a teacher workamommy who might be with him or might be just about anyw—

Stop it. Don't you let that rat out. That rat can do nothing but run, bite, and chase its own tail.

The plump woman, meanwhile, kept nodding. Her curls bounced along. "Yes, we've all lost someone, because this is the time of the great Tribulation. It's all in here, in Revelation." She held up the book she was carrying, and of course it was a Bible, and now Clay thought he was getting a better look at the sparkle in the eyes behind the plump woman cat's-eye glasses. That wasn't kindly interest; that was lunacy.

"Oh, that's it, everybody out of the pool," Tom said. In his voice Clay heard a mixture of disgust (at himself, for letting the plump woman bore in and get close to begin with, quite likely) and dismay.

The plump woman took no notice, of course; she had fixed Alice with her stare, and who was there to pull her away? The police were otherwise occupied, if there were any left. Here there were only the shocked and shuffling refugees, and they could care less about one elderly crazy lady with a Bible and a beauty-shop perm.

"The Vial of Insanity has been poured into the brains of the wicked, and the City of Sin has been set afire by the cleansing torch of Yee-*ho*-vah!" the plump lady cried. She was wearing red lipstick. Her teeth were too even to be anything but old-fashioned dentures. "Now you see the unrepentant flee, yea, verily, even as maggots flee the burst belly of—"

Alice put her hands over her ears. "Make her stop!" she cried, and still the ghost-shapes of the city's recent residents filed past, only a few sparing a dull, incurious glance before looking once more into the darkness where somewhere ahead New Hampshire lay.

The plump woman was starting to work up a sweat, Bible raised, eyes blazing, beauty-shop curls nodding and swaying. "Take your hands down, girl, and hear the Word of God before you let these men lead you away and fornicate with you in the open doorway of Hell itself! 'For I saw a star blaze in the sky, and it was called Wormwood, and those that followed it followed upon Lucifer, and those that followed upon Lucifer walked downward into the furnace of—' "

Clay hit her. He pulled the punch at the last second, but it was still a solid clip to the jaw, and he felt the impact travel all the way up to his shoulder. The plump woman's glasses rose off her pug nose and then settled back. Behind them, her eyes lost their glare and rolled up in their sockets. Her knees came unhinged and she buckled, her Bible tumbling from her clenched fist. Alice, still looking stunned and horrified, nevertheless dropped her hands from her ears fast enough to catch the Bible. And Tom McCourt caught the woman under her arms. The punch and the two subsequent catches were so neatly done they could have been choreographed.

Clay was suddenly closer to undone than at any time since things had started going wrong. Why this should have been worse than the throat-biting teenage girl or the knife-wielding businessman, worse than finding Mr. Ricardi hanging from a light fixture with a bag over his head, he didn't know, but it was. He had kicked the knife-wielding businessman, Tom had, too, but the knife-wielding businessman had been a different kind of crazy. The old lady with the beauty-shop curls had just been a . . .

"Jesus," he said. "She was just a nut, and I cold-cocked her." He was starting to shake.

"She was terrorizing a young girl who lost her mother today," Tom said, and Clay realized it wasn't calmness he heard in the small man's voice but an extraordinary coldness. "You did exactly the right thing. Besides, you can't keep an old iron horse like this down for long. She's coming around already. Help me get her over to the side of the road."

4

They had reached the part of Route One—sometimes called the Miracle Mile, sometimes Sleaze Alley—where limited-access highway yielded to a jostle of liquor marts, cut-rate clothing stores, sporting-goods outlets, and eateries with names like Fuddruckers. Here the six lanes were littered, if not quite choked, with vehicles that had either been piled up or just abandoned when their operators panicked, tried their cell phones, and went insane. The refugees wove their various courses silently among the remains, reminding Clay Riddell more than a little of ants evacuating a hill that has been demolished by the careless passing boot-stride of some heedless human.

There was a green reflectorized sign reading MALDEN SALEM ST. EXIT 1/4 MI at the edge of a low pink building that had been broken into; it was fronted by a jagged skirting of broken glass, and a battery-powered burglar alarm was even now in the tired last stages of running down. A glance at the dead sign on the roof was all Clay needed to tell him what had made the place a target in the aftermath of the day's disaster: MISTER BIG'S GIANT DISCOUNT LIQUOR.

He had one of the plump woman's arms. Tom had the other, and Alice supported the muttering woman's head as they eased her to a sitting position with her back against one of the exit sign's legs. Just as they got her down, the plump woman opened her eyes and looked at them dazedly.

Tom snapped his fingers in front of her eyes, twice, briskly. She blinked, then turned her eyes to Clay. "You . . . hit me," she said. Her fingers rose to touch the rapidly puffing spot on her jaw.

"Yes, I'm sor—" Clay began.

"He may be, but I'm not," Tom said. He spoke with that same cold briskness. "You were terrorizing our ward."

The plump woman laughed softly, but tears were in her eyes. "*Ward!* I've heard a lot of words for it, but never that one. As if I don't know what men like you want with a tender girl like this, especially in times like these. 'They repented not their fornications, nor their sodomies, nor their—' "

"Shut up," Tom said, "or I'll hit you myself. And unlike my friend, who was I think lucky enough not to grow up among the holy Hannahs and thus does not recognize you for what you are, I won't pull my punch. Fair warning—one more word." He held his fist before her eyes, and although Clay had already concluded that Tom was an educated man, civilized, and probably not much of a puncher under ordinary circumstances, he could not help feeling dismay at the sight of that small, tight fist, as if he were looking at an omen of the coming age.

The plump lady looked and said nothing. One large tear spilled down her rouged cheek.

"That's enough, Tom, I'm okay," Alice said.

Tom dropped the plump lady's shopping bag of possessions into her lap. Clay hadn't even realized Tom had salvaged it. Then Tom took the Bible from Alice, picked up one of the plump lady's be-ringed hands, and smacked the Bible into it, spine first. He started away, then turned back.

"Tom, that's enough, let's go," Clay said.

Tom ignored him. He bent toward the woman sitting with her back against the sign's leg. His hands were on his knees, and to Clay the two of them—the plump, spectacled woman looking up, the small, spectacled man bending over with his hands on his knees—looked like figures in some lunatic's parody of the early illustrations from the Charles Dickens novels.

"Some advice, sister," Tom said. "The police will no longer protect you as they did when you and your self-righteous, holy-rolling friends marched on the family planning centers or the Emily Cathcart Clinic in Waltham—"

"That abortion mill!" she spat, and then raised her Bible, as if to block a blow.

Tom didn't hit her, but he was smiling grimly. "I don't know about the Vial of Insanity, but there's certainly *beaucoup* crazy making the rounds tonight. May I be clear? The lions are out of their cages, and you may well find that they'll eat the mouthy Christians first. Somebody canceled your right of free speech around three o'clock this afternoon. Just a word to the wise." He looked from Alice to Clay, and Clay saw that the upper lip beneath the mustache was trembling slightly. "Shall we go?"

"Yes," Clay said.

"Wow," Alice said, once they were walking toward the Salem Street ramp again, Mister Big's Giant Discount Liquor falling behind them. "You grew up with someone like that?"

"My mother and both of her sisters," Tom said. "First N.E. Church of Christ the Redeemer. They took Jesus as their personal savior, and the church took them as its personal pigeons."

"Where is your mother now?" Clay asked.

Tom glanced at him briefly. "Heaven. Unless they rooked her on that one, too. I'm pretty sure the bastards did."

5

Near the stop sign at the foot of the ramp, two men were fighting over a keg of beer. If forced to guess, Clay would have said it had probably been liberated from Mister Big's Giant Discount Liquor. Now it lay forgotten against the guardrails, dented and leaking foam, while the two men—both brawny and both bleeding—battered each other with their fists. Alice shrank against him, and Clay put his arm around her, but there was something almost reassuring about these brawlers. They were angry—enraged—but not crazy. Not like the people back in the city.

One of them was bald and wearing a Celtics jacket. He hit the other a looping overhand blow that mashed his opponent's lips and knocked him flat. When the man in the Celtics jacket advanced on the downed man, the downed man scrambled away, then got up, still backing off. He spat blood. "Take it, ya fuck!" he yelled in a thick, weepy Boston accent. "Hope it chokes ya!"

The bald man in the Celtics jacket made as if to charge him, and the other went running up the ramp toward Route One. Celtics Jacket started to bend down for his prize, registered Clay, Alice, and Tom, and straightened up again. It was three to one, he had a black eye, and blood was trickling down the side of his face from a badly torn earlobe, but Clay saw no fear in that face, although he had only the diminishing light of the Revere fire to go by. He thought his grandfather would have said the guy's Irish was up, and certainly that went with the big green shamrock on the back of his jacket.

"The fuck you lookin at?" he asked.

"Nothing—just going by you, if that's all right," Tom said mildly. "I live on Salem Street."

"You can go to Salem Street or hell, far as I'm concerned," the bald man in the Celtics jacket said. "Still a free country, isn't it?"

"Tonight?" Clay said. "Too free."

The bald man thought it over and then laughed, a humorless double ha-ha. "The fuck happened? Any-a youse know?"

Alice said, "It was the cell phones. They made people crazy."

The bald man picked up the keg. He handled it easily, tipping it so the leak stopped. "Fucking things," he said. "Never cared to own one. Rollover minutes. The fuck're those?"

Clay didn't know. Tom might've—he'd owned a cell phone, so it seemed possible—but Tom said nothing. Probably didn't want to get into a long discussion with the bald man, and probably a good idea. Clay thought the bald man had some of the characteristics of an unexploded grenade.

"City burning?" the bald man asked. "Is, isn't it?"

"Yes," Clay said. "I don't think the Celtics will be playing at the Fleet this year."

"They ain't shit, anyway," the man said. "Doc Rivers couldn't coach a PAL team." He stood watching them, the keg on his shoulder, blood running down the side of his face. Yet now he seemed peaceable enough, almost serene. "Go on," he said. "But I wouldn't stay this close to the city for long. It's gonna get worse before it gets better. There's gonna be a lot more fires, for one thing. You think everybody who hightailed it north remembered to turn off the gas stove? I fuckin doubt it."

The three of them started walking, then Alice stopped. She pointed to the keg. "Was that yours?"

The bald man looked at her reasonably. "Ain't no was at times like this, sweetie pie. Ain't no was left. There's just now and maybe-tomorrow. It's mine now, and if there's any left it'll be mine maybe-tomorrow. Go on now. The fuck out."

"Seeya," Clay said, and raised one hand.

"Wouldn't want to be ya," the bald man replied, unsmiling, but he raised his own hand in return. They had passed the stop sign and were crossing to the far side of what Clay assumed was Salem Street when the bald man called after them again: "Hey, handsome!"

Both Clay and Tom turned to look, then glanced at each other, amused. The bald guy with the keg was now only a dark shape on the rising ramp; he could have been a caveman carrying a club.

"Where are the loonies now?" the bald guy asked. "You're not gonna tell me they're all dead, are ya? Cause I don't fuckin believe it."

"That's a very good question," Clay said.

"You're fuckin-A right it is. Watch out for the little sweetie pie there." And without waiting for them to reply, the man who'd won the battle of the beer keg turned and merged with the shadows.

6

"This is it," Tom said no more than ten minutes later, and the moon emerged from the wrack of cloud and smoke that had obscured it for the last hour or so as if the little man with the spectacles and the mustache had just given the Celestial Lighting Director a cue. Its rays—silver now instead of that awful infected orange—illuminated a house that was either dark blue, green, or perhaps even gray; without the streetlights to help, it was hard to tell for sure. What Clay *could* tell for sure was that the house was trim and handsome, although maybe not as big as your eye first insisted. The moonlight aided in that deception, but it was mostly caused by the way the steps rose from Tom McCourt's well-kept lawn to the only pillared porch on the street. There was a fieldstone chimney on the left. From above the porch, a dormer looked down on the street.

"Oh, Tom, it's *beautiful*!" Alice said in a too-rapturous voice. To Clay she sounded exhausted and bordering on hysteria. He himself didn't think it beautiful, but it certainly looked like the home of a man who owned a cell phone and all the other twenty-first-century bells and whistles. So did the rest of the houses on this part of Salem Street, and Clay doubted if many of the residents had had Tom's fantastic good luck. He looked around nervously. All the houses were dark—the power was out now—and they might have been deserted, except he seemed to feel eyes, surveying them.

The eyes of crazies? Phone-crazies? He thought of Power Suit Woman and Pixie Light; of the lunatic in the gray pants and the shredded tie; the man in the business suit who had bitten the ear right off the side of the dog's head. He thought of the naked man jabbing the car aerials back and forth as he ran. No, *surveying* was not in the phone-crazies' repertoire. They just came at you. But if there were normal people holed up in these houses—*some* of them, anyway—where *were* the phone-crazies?

Clay didn't know.

"I don't know if I'd exactly call it beautiful," Tom said, "but it's still standing, and that's good enough for me. I'd pretty well made up my mind that we'd get here and find nothing but a smoking hole in the ground." He reached in his pocket and brought out a slim ring of keys. "Come on in. Be it ever so humble, and all that."

They started up the walk and had gone no more than half a dozen steps when Alice cried, *"Wait!"*

Clay wheeled around, feeling both alarm and exhaustion. He thought he was beginning to understand combat fatigue a little. Even his adrenaline felt tired. But no one was there—no phone-crazies, no bald man with blood flowing down the side of his face from a shredded ear, not even a little old lady with the talkin apocalypse blues. Just Alice, down on one knee at the place where Tom's walk left the sidewalk.

"What is it, honey?" Tom asked.

She stood up, and Clay saw she was holding a very small sneaker. "It's a Baby Nike," she said. "Do you—"

Tom shook his head. "I live alone. Except for Rafe, that is. He thinks he's the king, but he's only the cat."

"Then who left it?" She looked from Tom to Clay with wondering, tired eyes.

Clay shook his head. "No telling, Alice. Might as well toss it."

But Clay knew she would not; it was déjà vu at its

disorienting worst. She still held it in her hand, curled against her waist, as she went to stand behind Tom, who was on the steps, picking slowly through his keys in the scant light.

Now we hear the cat, Clay thought. *Rafe.* And sure enough, there was the cat that had been Tom McCourt's salvation, *waowing* a greeting from inside.

7

Tom bent down and Rafe or Rafer—both short for Rafael—leaped into his arms, purring loudly and stretching his head up to sniff Tom's carefully trimmed mustache.

"Yeah, missed you, too," Tom said. "All is forgiven, believe me." He carried Rafer across the enclosed porch, stroking the top of his head. Alice followed. Clay came last, closing the door and turning the knob on the lock before catching up to the others.

"Follow along down to the kitchen," Tom said when they were in the house proper. There was a pleasant smell of furniture polish and, Clay thought, leather, a smell he associated with men living calm lives that did not necessarily include women. "Second door on the right. Stay close. The hallway's wide, and there's nothing on the floor, but there are tables on both sides and it's as black as your hat. As I think you can see."

"So to speak," Clay said.

"Ha-ha."

"Have you got flashlights?" Clay asked.

"Flashlights and a Coleman lantern that should be even better, but let's get in the kitchen first."

They followed him down the hallway, Alice walking between the two men. Clay could hear her breathing rapidly, trying not to let the unfamiliar surroundings freak her out, but of course it was hard. Hell, it was hard for him. Disorienting. It would have been better if there had been even a little light, but—

His knee bumped one of the tables Tom had mentioned, and something that sounded all too ready to break rattled like teeth. Clay steeled himself for the smash, and for Alice's scream. That she *would* scream was almost a given. Then whatever it was, a vase or some knickknack, decided to live a little longer and settled back into place. Still, it seemed like a very long walk before Tom said, "Here, okay? Hard right."

The kitchen was nearly as black as the hall, and Clay had just a moment to think of all the things he was missing and Tom must be missing more: a digital readout on the microwave oven, the hum of the fridge, maybe light from a neighboring house coming in through the window over the kitchen sink and making highlights on the faucet.

"Here's the table," Tom said. "Alice, I'm going to take your hand. Here's a chair, okay? I'm sorry if I sound like we're playing blindman's bluff."

"It's all r—," she began, then gave a little scream that made Clay jump. His hand was on the haft of his knife (now he thought of it as his) before he even realized he'd reached for it.

"What?" Tom asked sharply. *"What?"*

"Nothing," she said. "Just . . . nothing. The cat. His tail . . . on my leg."

"Oh. I'm sorry."

"It's all right. *Stupid,*" she added with self-contempt that made Clay wince in the dark.

"No," he said. "Let up on yourself, Alice. It's been a tough day at the office."

"Tough day at the office!" Alice repeated, and laughed in a way Clay didn't care for. It reminded him of her voice when she'd called Tom's house beautiful. He thought, *That's going to get away from her, and then what do I do? In the movies the hysterical girl gets a slap across the chops and it always brings her around, but in the movies you can see where she* is.

He didn't have to slap her, shake her, or hold her, which was what he probably would have tried first. She heard what was in her own voice, maybe, got hold of it, and bulldogged it down: first to a choked gargle, then to a gasp, then to quiet.

"Sit," Tom said. "You have to be tired. You too, Clay. I'll get us some light."

Clay felt for a chair and sat down to a table he could hardly see, although his eyes had to be fully adjusted to the dark by now. There was a whisper of something against his pants leg, there and gone. A low miaow. Rafe.

"Hey, guess what?" he said to the dim shape of the girl as Tom's footsteps receded. "Ole Rafer just put a jump in me, too." Although he hadn't, not really.

"We have to forgive him," she said. "Without that cat, Tom would be just as crazy as the rest of them. And that would be a shame."

"It would."

"I'm so scared," she said. "Do you think it will get better tomorrow, in the daylight? The being scared part?"

"I don't know."

"You must be worried sick about your wife and little boy."

Clay sighed and rubbed his face. "The hard part is trying to come to grips with the helplessness. We're sep-